Secrets with the Marquess

REGENCY IN COLOR BOOK 10

CECILIA RENE

For more information about the author: www.ceciliareneauthor.com

Twitter: @cecilia_rene

Facebook: cecilia rene

Instagram: authorceciliarene

TicTok: @authorceciliarene

Website: ceciliareneauthor.com

Edited by Wendy Muruli, Tessera Editorial

Proofread by Prose without Thorns

Cover Design by Erin Dameron-Hill, edh Graphics

Formatting by Colorful Pen Press Inc

Dedicated to my Aunt Ruby.
Tolbert, I know you're looking down at us all from your seat next to Jesus and smiling.

Chapter One

T he cold, brisk wind swirled around Journey Beaumont, making her long, green cloak whirl around her limbs. She shivered, feeling the chill down to her bones, but she didn't care. It had been a fortnight of nothing but frigid, dreary rain, and both she and her pupil needed a reprieve. It was a clear, crisp Spring Day in Wales, one that begged them to venture out from the confines of Plas Castle.

Taking a deep inhale, Journey allowed the fresh air to rejuvenate her after a restless night of no sleep. She had four months remaining until she would be free, free from running and hiding, free to return to Jamaica. After the death of her father two years earlier, Journey had planned to return home, but her father's business partner had other plans for her.

Bernard Ramsay and her father had been the best of friends. They had owned a shipping company specializing in human cargo for many years, a fact that Journey was not proud of in the least. Mr. Ramsay felt that as her father's closest friend, he should have inherited everything that Martin Beaumont owned, but her father had felt differently. He'd left everything to his only child, Journey.

Another cool breeze assaulted her, blowing thick, curly hair in her face. It had taken Journey an immense amount of time to become accustomed to the English and Welsh climate. She had lived the first seven years of her life in Jamaica where the weather was so hot you could not help but dream of running deep into the chaotic arms of the ocean. The heat clung to the skin like crystallized sugar cane, making it impossible not to sweat as if you were hugging the sun. She missed the warm sun, clear skies, and palm trees so tall she felt they could reach heaven. Although it had not been her home for many years, if Journey closed her eyes, she could still see miles and miles of fields filled with sugar cane. The immaculate white house where she was born stood sentry over the plantation, a symbol of power and dominance.

A symbol she was determined to destroy.

"Miss Beaumont!" her young charge, Lady Emma Huxley, called excitedly. "I picked these especially for you." Emma was a beautiful little girl with pale skin, dark eyes, and wild, dark hair. It wasn't like Journey's array of coarse, tight curls that hung to her shoulders; Emma's silky hair was long and luxurious, proof of her Welsh ancestry.

She ran toward Journey, holding a pitiful bunch of wild primrose that were plucked too soon. It was the beginning of spring in Wales, but Mother Nature was clutching the last remnants of winter like it was her favorite child.

"They're beautiful, luv, but perhaps we should let them grow more before we snatch them from nature." Journey bent, taking the small bushel in her hands and making a show of sniffing. The sweet floral scent filled her nostrils, and she couldn't help but close her eyes, wishing for warmer days.

"I know, but I truly wanted to do something nice for you since you're always so nice to me." Emma nodded her head, ending the conversation.

A small smile crept at the corner of Journey's mouth; it was easy to be kind to the thoughtful little girl. She'd found that she loved her instantly and feared breaking her own heart when she finally would have to leave in four months. She tried to ignore Emma's resemblance to her father, but there was no denying the perfectly symmetrical face of the Marquess of Aberdeen.

Her employer, Archibald Huxley, was devastatingly handsome, a wonderful father and, for lack of a better phrase, a complete horse's ass. From the moment the Dowager of Aberdeen hired her six months prior, Journey and the marquess had fought constantly over everything. The man felt it was his personal responsibility to criticize her over every single detail. She wouldn't have minded if it was only over Emma's tutelage, but no, it was everything. Anything that he thought was not acceptable for a governess in his employ to do, say, think, or wear.

Forcing herself to not think of the infuriating yet handsome man, she'd tried to avoid him every single day since she arrived in Wales. *Four months*, she repeated to herself. Journey had 142 days before she could leave the marquess' employ. Her only regret would be that she would have to part with Emma, whom she had grown to love more than anything.

"Let's head back to the Castle, luv. The weather is growing frigid." Journey pulled the green cloak tighter around her, waiting patiently for Emma, who was running in the wind.

Emma was an energetic child that reminded Journey of herself at that age. It was a time in her life when she had been young and blissfully ignorant of the truth.

"Can we stay out a little longer? It's been raining forever," Emma protested, dark eyes blinking up at Journey.

"We will come back out tomorrow. We must prepare ourselves for dinner." Journey clenched her teeth tight, afraid that if she said more, she would reveal how she truly felt about dinner.

The marquess insisted she dined with him and Emma every evening. Journey usually tried to spend her time conversing with Emma on any and everything, but he always inserted himself into their conversations. She had to admit that seeing a man of his wealth and nobility take such a great interest in his daughter was moving.

Emma took Journey's hand, swinging her arm back and forth happily as they made their way back to the Castle. Plas Castle sat nestled atop of a hill overlooking Snowdonia, in Harlech. The Snowdonia Mountains cast their enormous shadows in the distance. Everywhere Journey turned, nature surrounded her. It was beautiful, covered by marshland and greenery. The small village of Harlech bustled beneath them.

Journey had loved her grandmother's home, Heartstone Park, where she'd lived most of her life until she had to leave two years ago. However, there was something about Plas Castle that called to her as if it was where she was meant to be. The ancient structure with lush grounds, tall towers, and weathered bricks felt like home to her. It was like being back in Jamaica in her mother's arms, safe and secure. Emma's home had become her own, but it was a thought Journey did not wish to linger on for too long.

"Emma, can you help me?" Journey asked, starting the familiar game the two of them played together.

"Of course," the girl answered happily, her resemblance to her father overwhelming.

"I can't remember what country we're in." Journey tapped her lips with her free gloved hand.

"You're in Wales, silly." Emma laughed as they made their way back up the hill of the castle. Journey held her hand, knowing how steep the climb would be, though they never ventured far.

"Wales? How extraordinary! I dreamed I was in France. *Je m'appelle*, Journey." Entering the grounds, its inhabitants immediately met them going about their day, all at the behest of the marquess.

"*Moi, c'est* Emma," the girl replied in a more appropriate French accent.

They had been practicing for months, starting with the alphabet, pronunciation, days of the week, and months of the year. Now they were onto phrases.

Being a governess was the last thing Journey had planned to do. She had intended to spend her life fighting for those oppressed, like so many of her family members and those of African descent did. Once her father died, the universe had other plans for her, ones that she did not agree with at all.

They walked into the castle, hand in hand, entering the north side of the home. This was Journey's least favorite part of the castle; it was impersonal and cold with its wall-to-wall paintings of Welsh ancestors followed by freshly gleamed knights in armor who greeted them as they strolled down the long hallways.

"Thank heavens, you two have returned!" the house-keeper, Mrs. Caddick, called, running toward Journey and Emma. "The marquess is in an uproar, Miss Beaumont. He wants to see you in his study straight away. I'll take Miss Emma upstairs to Agnes." The housekeeper rambled like she was rushing to save Wales from another invasion.

Journey liked Mrs. Caddick. She was efficient and straight-forward, and she never minced words. The woman told you exactly what she felt. After growing up with her grandmother, Journey appreciated that quality in anyone. Her only problem with Mrs. Caddick was that the woman treated the marquess like he was a god, and he was only a man. The most infuriating but devilishly handsome man she had ever met in her entire life but still just a man.

"Miss Beaumont, are you in trouble?" Emma asked, her eyes watering slightly.

"Never you mind, Lady Emma." Mrs. Caddick reprimanded Emma, clucking like a hen.

Journey bent down to address the little girl. "I could never be in trouble, luv." She pinched Emma's cheek. "And if I ever were, I will always get out of it." She winked for good measure, but inside she was preparing for a battle.

Who knew what the marquess was vexed about now?

"Yes, but try to mind yourself. It does not help you fighting him on every subject." Mrs. Caddick squeezed Journey's arm. "You're too strong," she said in a thick Welsh accent.

Journey stood, smiling at the woman. "It's the only way I know how to be." With those last words, she walked down the hall, going to face him.

The closer she was to his study, the more her body vibrated in anticipation, her stomach clenching in that familiar way it had done every day since she had arrived six months ago.

Journey ignored it. He was her employer; he could be nothing else.

Her life's mission was oceans away, and she would do nothing to jeopardize her plans.

She had been hiding for two years, and it was almost over. Besides, she was an employee, a servant in his eyes. Nothing would happen between them. Journey could do nothing that would reveal her before her twenty-first birthday. Not even give herself over to the most delicious man she had ever beheld.

Chapter Two

Archibald Peregrine Huxley, The Sixth Marquess of Aberdeen, sat in his pristine study with his fingers entwined, waiting impatiently for his daughter's governess. Slow inhales and exhales moved his entire body up and down. His eyes surveyed the details of the cluttered space. An extensive collection on poetry, dictionaries from all over the world, an entire bookshelf dedicated to Shakespeare, vases, chests, and cabinets.

Dark furniture decorated the large space. A burgundy sofa and matching chaise lounge sat against the wall. Welsh oak bookcases covered every wall, filled with Archie's entire collection of books. There was no corner left unnoticed, as he would do anything to keep his mind off the woman that had consumed his every thought since she first arrived.

Shifting the papers on his desk, he ignored every part of his body that came alive at the thought of seeing Miss Beaumont. It did not matter how she made him feel; she was not for him. It was a fact that Archie reminded himself of daily. Miss Beaumont was in his employ and therefore under his protection. She was an unmarried woman in a strange country, thousands of miles from home, and he would be a cad to take advantage of the situation.

Although Archie would never forget his late wife, Katherine, and the love they shared, after nine long years without her, it was time for him to move on. Their daughter needed a mother, and he needed a wife.

His eyes fell upon the letter from his mother, taking in her sugary sweet words.

"So very pleased that you and Emma will arrive for the season. After all, you promised your Mama."

Archie regretted that promise now that it was March, and the season would begin soon.

He knew that Katherine would want him to marry and be happy, and he wanted it too. Creamy brown skin, wild dark hair, and light-brown eyes that were kissed by the sun flashed in his mind. He ignored the images, closing his eyes and willing the tempting mirage of her away.

There had been women he'd found attractive since Katherine's death, but no one had lit a fire in his veins until Journey Beaumont stepped inside of Plas Castle.

Archie wasn't blind. He was a fully grown man with needs, needs that had not been fulfilled in years. Miss Beaumont was an attractive woman. Heads turned when she waltzed into a room. It was the only word that described how she moved. Her wide hips glided smoothly; it was mesmerizing to behold. She had captured his attention the moment she stepped into his study. Silky brown skin, a long sensual neck, and a full bosom. They started from her slim waist, curving out voluptuous and full. The sight of her always left him speechless for long moments at a time.

Hell and damnation, he was hard just thinking about the first time he saw her. She wasn't a doe-eyed debutante or a soft-spoken bluestocking—she was Cleopatra reborn, fierce, and wonderfully made. Archie tried everything to quell his attraction, but nothing sated him.

Sighing, Archie looked back down at his mother's letter, moving it to the side to reveal another from his closest friend, The Duke of Richmore. A pang of guilt and shame filled him as his eyes scanned over the letter begging him to come to Parliament and participate in the abolition movement again.

He had done his part in 1807 and paid a great price for it. Archie joined Parliament a year after his father's death. At twenty, he was young and hungry for change. Richmore was a young duke; they had been acquaintances at university together, but it was fighting to end the slave trade that united them forever. They did it. Along with the other abolitionist, and the main supporters of the Slave Trade Act, they ended the transatlantic slave trade. Though Archie came in only two years earlier, he had felt as victorious as though he had started the fight in the 1700s.

Now years later, he saw his mistakes, knew what it had cost him. There was no more fighting for him. He had done his part.

Running his hand through his thick, dark hair, he knew he had no choice but to participate in the upcoming London Season. If for nothing else but to cleanse his mind of the goddess that was Miss Journey Beaumont. A thousand scenarios on how to rid himself of the blasted woman ran rampant in his mind often, but there was nothing to be done. Sending her back to the England was out of the question. His mother had hired Miss Beaumont directly from a prominent Ladies' Seminary, so there was nothing in her education that would cause her to be terminated. Besides, she was excellent with Emma. In the short time she'd had with her, his daughter had grown tremendously in both education and in spirits.

Although Miss Beaumont was an excellent governess to his daughter, Archie felt she was hiding something. She rarely spoke of her past, claiming that she was an orphan taken in by the school's mistress who was a friend of her mother's. Yet every article of clothing Miss Beaumont owned was above her supposed station. Archie was not a connoisseur of women's clothing, but he knew hers were of the finest quality, muslin, cotton, and even satin. Her manners were immaculate, speech perfect. There was nothing about her that said she'd had a strenuous life as most orphans had. No, he did not believe the story at all. He knew Miss Beaumont was hiding something, and he would discover the truth.

Archie's obsession with Miss Beaumont was bothersome to him. She had been in his employ for six agonizing months, and there wasn't a day that went by that he did not think about her or want to drop to his knees and beg her to allow him to worship at her altar. He did not know how he was going to survive years with the antagonizing goddess living in his home.

A knock on the door jolted him to sit upright. Swallowing several times, he intertwined his fingers once more. If they were occupied, there was no fear he would do something juvenile like touch her.

How he wanted to, so badly.

"Enter." His voice was void of all emotion. He had become a theater actor in a matter of months.

Dear God, he should be on stage.

The door opened slowly, so tardily that he wanted to scream at it, demand it reveal her to him, to wrestle with the blasted door for keeping such a wondrous sight from his eyes.

Walking over the threshold into his study, Journey Beaumont glided on a magical carpet, her hips swinging side to side through the thick wool of her cloak. Smooth brown skin was damp with perspiration from the heat in the castle, as if she had over exhausted herself. Archie could think of many ways that he wanted to over exhaust her. However, that was not why she was there.

Licking his dry lips, he tried to be the professional employer that he was required to be, but it was rather difficult when she walked into his study looking like a goddess.

"You wanted to see me, my lord?" Her voice was husky and deep.

Archie inhaled deeply, savoring the burn in his lungs for several minutes before he released the breath, allowing his nerves to calm before he spoke. "Did you take my daughter outside today?"

Miss Beaumont eyed him, her face stoic and unreadable, but he could see the inner workings of her thoughts. "Clearly," she said, motioning to her cloaked body.

The gesture gave him the opportunity to ogle her freely, and he took his fill of her, noticing how the cape rested on each glorious inch of her.

Ignoring her snide comment, Archie continued. "Have I not informed you that I do not want Lady Emma out in the cold? She is still quite young, and I do not want her becoming ill." It was an accurate statement. After his wife's death, Archie found himself rather paranoid when it came to Emma and his mother's health.

They were his only living relatives after all, and he did not want to lose them as he had lost both his father and Katherine.

Miss Beaumont pinched her lips, her eyes liquid pools of fire. "Yes, and I have informed you that I am the governess, and as the governess I feel that venturing outdoors is key to one's constitution—"

"I don't care—"

"I'm not finished." They spoke over each other, eyes locked in a heated gaze.

Archie's blood boiled. He was both upset by her insolent

behavior and completely aroused that she had the gall to stand up to him in his own study.

He was a man accustomed to always getting his way. People listened when he talked, followed his every command, except her. Miss Beaumont did not listen to him, did not work to please him as her employer, or follow his instructions regarding the care of his daughter.

Miss Beaumont held up her index finger as she continued, indicating that Archie had rudely interrupted her. "Not only is fresh air and exercise beneficial to young ladies, but we also learn as we venture around the grounds. After being imprisoned in the castle for a sennight, I decided as her governess that we should venture outdoors."

Having had enough of her sanctimonious speech, Archie stood, walking around the large oak desk, sliding in front of her to lean against it. He was an arm's length away. The urge to reach out and wrap his arms around her small waist to bring her luscious body flush against his was nearly overwhelming, but he resisted.

"I understand you are the governess, but I am her only surviving parent, and I expect you to follow my instructions as your employer." Archie gripped the desk tighter, willing himself not to do anything untoward. Yes, Miss Beaumont was a beautiful woman, but she was also his employee. She should be safe in his house and in his presence.

He was a gentleman after all.

Archie came from a long line of gentlemen, men who treasured honor above anything else. His grandfather was Welsh and had quickly pledged his allegiance to King Edward I. Every man in his family put duty and honor first, so surely he could exemplify the same behavior and not give in to this wild attraction he had for the woman in front of him.

Miss Beaumont gave him a tight smile that did not reach her light-brown eyes. "We agreed when I first arrived at Plas

Castle that you would allow me the freedom to choose Lady Emma's curriculum. Has that changed in any way?" she asked, tipping her head to the side and blinking repeatedly. It was a mocking gesture, he knew, but he couldn't deny how adorable she was. "We were only out for half an hour today. In that span of time, we covered the country and French and picked flowers, although they are not fully in bloom since the weather is still frigid. We also discussed the nearest body of water. It was a learning adventure that allowed Emma to break free from the confines of the castle."

Archie sighed in frustration, not wanting to agree with the exasperating woman. "I don't want my daughter out in this weather for too long. Half an hour maximum, and she must be covered to protect against the elements."

"Indeed, I will. Please remember, my lord, that I love Lady Emma as if she was my very own. I would do nothing that would put her in harm's way."

Her sincere words pierced his dormant heart.

Of course, he had noticed her connection to his daughter. A connection that was stolen from his late wife the moment their daughter was born. But that was not Miss Beaumont's fault, and in fact, he was grateful that the woman was so warm and welcoming with his daughter.

"Please clear every outing with me first." He forced the words out, fighting with his baser instincts.

"If that is what you wish." Miss Beaumont forced a smile on her full lips.

"It is. For her safety and yours, I would like to know before you venture outdoors." Archie watched as Miss Beaumont's armor showed signs of weakness, her eyes losing their fire at his words.

Was she surprised that he would consider her safety?

Of course, he would. Not only was she in his employ, but

his daughter loved her, and he...Archie ignored the stinging in his chest at the thought of anything befalling Miss Beaumont.

"I-Is there anything else, Lord Aberdeen?" she asked, her voice trembling for some unknown reason.

"Yes." Archie stood, making the space between them smaller. He could smell her fragrance, and it was unlike anything he had ever smelled before. It was sweet and spicy. "We will leave for London in a fortnight. Please have Lady Emma prepared."

Archie watched as Miss Beaumont took a shaky step back, nearly losing her balance. Without thinking, he wrapped his hands around her waist, steadying her. "Are you all right?" She had gone pale, her eyes wide in fear.

"I'm well, just lightheaded." She touched the back of her hand to her forehead.

Leading her to the nearest chair, Archie urged her to sit as he knelt in front of her. Cupping her cheek, he searched her face for any signs of pain or discomfort. Her eyes captured his, the heat from her soft skin scorching his hand. Archie knew he should remove it, but he couldn't. It was the first time that he had ever touched her, and good God, he wanted more.

Chapter Three

Heat, security, comfort, and want swirled through Journey as she stayed locked in the marquess's gaze. He was touching her, and she was allowing him to. It was innocent as far as touches went, but she could feel it everywhere like she was bare in front of him. Journey had been empty for so long that she had not remembered what it was like to feel anything.

Staring into his blue eyes, ones that reminded her of the Caribbean Sea, she wanted to swim in them forever. She could not think of anything other than him. It was strange: from the moment she had arrived, they had been at odds over Emma's teachings, but even then, she felt his fire, and she knew if she touched it, she would burn.

Aberdeen licked his lips, drawing Journey's attention. The top one was slightly thinner than the bottom, and she had an insurmountable urge to press her lips against them. His eyes went to her lips, and in that moment, she knew if she didn't stop it she may live to regret it.

Journey stood abruptly, forcing the marquess to his feet, officially releasing herself from the hypnotizing trance. She released the stuttering breath that was lodged in her throat, her entire body shaking in want and in fear. Fear because she almost forgot her purpose, the reason she was there at all.

"Are you sure you're well?" he asked, starting toward her, but she stepped back, coming in contact with the desk, knocking the papers off and causing them to fall to the lush, embroidered carpet.

"Apologies, my lord." Journey bent down to retrieve the scattered papers, wanting to flee the suffocating study.

She was a disaster in that moment and had nearly ruined everything. Being Lady Emma's governess was the perfect position for her, and she needed its security just a little longer. It would not help to do anything untoward with her employer.

"N-no, please allow me, Miss Beaumont." He bent down in front of her, gathering the papers. His free hand touched her gloved one, and all she felt was fire.

Journey tried to ignore the heat radiating between them, the air crackling with tension. She could feel every part of him...and she wanted him. She had no choice but to ignore her own body's response, the thumping of her heart, the small birds fluttering in her abdomen. She couldn't give in to him. Her family depended on her, and she would not fail them.

Reaching for a pamphlet just under the desk, she grabbed it before standing. She fisted the small bound book in her hands, using it as a shield. "I-I really must be going."

"Please allow me to apologize if I've offended you." The marquess's sincere apology and softness took her by surprise.

Journey had only seen one side of him, the scowling, argumentative side that she faced daily. This gentler marquess who stood in front of her full of concern was a complete surprise, and she did not know how to react to his behavior. When he was angry or making a rude remark, it was easy to meet fire with fire, but this terrified her. He had a softness toward her that she had never seen before, his eyes full of emotion, his body vibrating with heat. She wanted to claim it as her own, bask in it like it was the sun after a wintry day.

Journey loosened her hold on the pamphlet, looking down at the object in her hand. She needed something to stare at other than the blue-eyed man in front of her. Blinking several times, she couldn't register what it was she was seeing on the thick printed paper.

An African man wearing nothing but a cloth around his lower half was bent on one knee, begging, or praying with chains on his wrists and arms. It was a heartbreaking image, one that took her very breath away. With trembling hands, Journey caressed the black-and-white portrayal of bondage. Her mouth gaped open to accommodate the sudden onslaught of breath that couldn't come out fast enough. Tears of hopelessness pooled then fell freely down her face, and she could do nothing to stop them.

The pamphlet was a reminder of her cause, of the people who needed her back home in Jamaica. The drawing felt so real that she felt the man could jump off the page and walk out of bondage. Journey knew that the only thing that separated her from those in bondage were their births. Had she been born on the other side of the blanket she too would be a slave.

"Dear God, I didn't mean for it to upset you." The marquess gently reached for the pamphlet in her hand, but she pulled it away.

She read the words on the cover before flipping open the booklet. "Are they trying to abolish slavery?" she asked, her eyes furiously taking in the information.

Aberdeen nodded before placing the other papers back on his desk. "Yes, that has always been our goal—"

"Our?" Journey asked, shocked by his words. She didn't believe that he was the sort of man who would fight for those oppressed. He was wealthy and titled. How could he empathize with the enslaved man, let alone fight for him? The world was at his feet. How much could he know of the oppressed?

"Yes, I was a part of the abolitionist movement when I was younger. Richmore and I fought tirelessly to end the slave trade, and now he wants us to continue what we started all those years ago." He ran his hand through his dark tresses, his eyes looking haunted and afraid.

"And you do not wish to continue fighting?" She tried to hide the anger in her voice, but it was impossible.

She would never stop fighting for freedom and equality for those oppressed and mistreated. It was always who she was meant to be.

"No, I've done my part. It's over. The slave trade ended—"

Journey shook her head, unable to be quiet. "It's not over! That was one minute part of the entire system." She held up the pamphlet, shaking it like a flag. "Bravo, you all stopped the abduction of innocent people from their homeland, but now what? It's been ten years, and hundreds of thousands, maybe even millions of people of African descent are still not free."

The marquess pushed himself off the desk, towering over her. She could see that she had upset him. *Good. He needed to be upset if he thought the work was done.*

"I'm aware, but ending the slave trade cut their resources at the root." He slammed his fist against his open palm. She watched, enthralled by the small spark of passion she saw. "They can no longer travel to West Central Africa or Senegambia and steal innocent people from their lives, their families. No more horror stories of hundreds of enslaved men and women lost at sea. That was a success, Miss Beaumont."

Journey took a deep inhale, ignoring his masculine scent. "It was a success, but what's next?" She tilted her head, observing him for a moment. He was at a loss for words, bringing his hand up to stroke his bare chin. "It'll never be over until every man, woman, and child is f-free." Her words were stuck in her throat as a wave of grief attacked her. She felt so helpless in that moment and wanted desperately to do something, anything, to help. "If I could..." She tapped her chest repeatedly. "...free an entire race of people, I would never stop fighting."

The tears fell freely, her chest aching with the weight of thousands of people. There was nothing but the sound of heavy breathing, and Journey could not fathom if it was coming from him or her. Journey held out the pamphlet, needing to escape the onslaught of emotions that had attacked her. She needed air and to be away from him.

Journey let out a gasp as one of Aberdeen's hands cupped her cheek, his thumb wiping her tears away. Her overheated body trembled from his rough but gentle touch, the gentle gesture soothing her battered emotions.

"I can't fight anymore—I lost..." He didn't continue his sentence, dropping his hand from her cheek and freeing her once again from his spell. Journey cleared her throat before reaching to place the pamphlet on his desk. Aberdeen took hold of her wrist, shaking his head. "Keep it."

She nodded, wiping her own tears with her gloved hand before she turned to walk away, but paused. "There is a difference between you and I..." She held his gaze, wanting him to understand.

"What is that?" he asked, his deep and raspy voice causing her abdomen to flutter.

"You can choose to stop fighting, but I don't have a choice."

Journey walked out of his study with her head held high. It must have been nice to choose one's fate. The color of her skin took that choice away from her.

Weaving through the long-adorned halls of the castle, she willed her legs to move faster, needing to be alone with her thoughts and emotions. The events of the afternoon had turned in so many ways that she was not expecting. He had touched her, and that simple act excited her. She knew she could never give in to the symphony of feelings that he had caused in only a few brief minutes.

Journey gripped the pamphlet tightly against her chest, a constant reminder of what she was fighting for. Her booted feet slapped the marble floor as she sped through the castle, heart pounding, breath panting. Her thighs ached from the pace she was setting. Journey cursed their size for once in her life, wishing that her legs were more muscular to carry her to the safety of her rooms faster. Distance, she needed blessed space between her and the marquess.

Weaving through the castle, she passed century-old paintings, vases dating back to the fifteenth century, and servants staring strangely at her.

Reaching the west wing where her rooms were located nearly caused Journey to relax, but there would be no peace until she was safely locked away. She had not intended to lose her temper or show emotion with her employer. They had a history of bickering, but everything that had happened in his study felt different, felt like *more*.

His touch had provoked her, and she hated to admit that she wanted him to touch her again. Journey's overheated body was buzzing with a million sensations. The pounding in her chest was evidence that the marquess affected her greatly.

Journey had not been prepared for Lord Aberdeen to stand so near or to touch her, and for an infinitesimal moment or two, she had wanted to press her lips against his and forget everything. But she could not, and his refusal to continue the fight against slavery was a harsh reminder of their differences.

Finally reaching her room, she ran behind the safety of the large oak door, pressing her back against it. She sighed, closing her eyes, gripping the pamphlet so tightly that she heard the paper crinkling in the palm of her hands.

She could never stop fighting for freedom for those that were in bondage, like her family in Jamaica. Journey knew the truth of slavery firsthand. She had seen it as a little girl—people working night and day in the blistering sun not by choice but because they were owned by her family, by her father, and soon they would all be owned by her.

She could not stop fighting. Everything depended on her remaining hidden. There were people who were relying on Journey for their freedom, and she could not risk being found.

Journey had to do everything in her power to ensure that Bernard Ramsay never would discover where she was hidden.

Chapter Four

In the sennight since his confrontation with Miss Beaumont, Archie lost himself in the minute details of preparing for the upcoming London departure. There were several things that required his attention since there was no marchioness to oversee them. Archie needed to ensure that they had enough carriages and horses for the journey. He had to select a small number of servants to travel with them. The London townhome had a small staff in residence. He saw no reason to have a full staff year-round in London when he primarily lived in Wales and rarely visited Town.

After Katherine's sudden death, Archie spent years mourning her, refusing to leave the familiar walls of the castle, a place she had loved. It wasn't just Katherine that held him to Plas. It was also filled with memories of his childhood. Of walking the snowy hills with his father every winter until his death. The castle wasn't his family's only ancestral home. In truth, the estate in Sussex was the family seat, but it was Plas Castle that claimed his heart and soul.

Archie ran his hands through his thick, dark hair, noting his reflection in the mirror as his valet, Howard, stood to the side, tying his cravat for dinner. He was in desperate need of a haircut and would need a proper one before he entered the London season in search of a wife.

After his indiscretion with Miss Beaumont, Archie was convinced now more than ever that it was time for him to find a suitable bride. Not only had he upset her with his ignorant comments on the abolition movement, but he had also touched her. Not once but twice did his hands make direct contact with her skin, which was soft and inviting. He found it difficult to forget how it felt to have her warm flesh beneath his calloused fingertips. When she spoke of fighting for slavery, it moved him so much that he wished he could continue to battle as he had done as a younger man.

He was a man of two and thirty, and he knew the cost of throwing yourself into a cause. No matter how noble and good, there was always a price.

"My lord?" Howard held out his tailcoat, waiting for Archie to place his arms in the sleeves.

Slipping his arm through the fabric, he tried not to let his mind stray to the beautiful brown-skinned woman with a fierce passion for justice. Archie's mind had been so occupied with thinking about Miss Beaumont...*Journey*. Her words had awoken a long-buried feeling inside him. Archie had lost the eagerness and determination it took to fight in the long war on slavery, but her passionate words moved him, and he wished he could do more. However, he was afraid of what he would lose.

Once Howard finished making sure Archie was free of all lint and wrinkles, Archie checked his reflection one last time before walking out of his rooms. The incessant beating of his heart and the tightness of his abdomen were all signs of his anticipation in seeing Miss Beaumont again. They had avoided each other the past eight days except at dinners where they sat in silence, allowing Emma to carry the conversation between them.

It was difficult to be in the same room with Miss Beaumont. He wanted to talk more about her beliefs and passion, to discover what else lit a fire in her soul. But Archie knew that wanting more from her was not ideal. He could still see the image of her enraged and standing firmly in his mind daily. When he closed his eyes, all he saw was her passion and determination, and she was breathtaking with tears streaming down her beautiful face. For the first time in over nine years, he wanted to fight to be worthy of her.

Archie hadn't had the urge to battle for anything in so many years that it felt foreign and out of place to him. Yet he found himself looking at the other information that Richmore had sent him on the movement. Fear and dread had crept up his spine, reminding him of what he'd lost.

He was no longer that young man eager for justice. He was a father, a landlord, and a damn fine horseman. There was no room in his life for a cause. No, Archie would let others fight for freedom.

Stopping in front of Emma's room, he knocked, waiting patiently until her maid, Agnes, opened the door, dipping a curtsey before she stepped aside, revealing his daughter.

"Papa! You look dashing." Emma skipped toward him, her dark curls bouncing with every step. She was his replica. They had the same hair and nose, but her mouth and dark eyes were completely her mother's. Whenever she smiled, he saw Katherine shining through.

"Thank you, *fy mach i*," he told her affectionately, calling her *his little one* as he had done her entire life. "You look beautiful." He offered her his arm, and Emma took it eagerly.

Archie had made it a habit to escort Emma to dinner every night. It had only been the two of them for so long he saw no need to go by the rules of society in his house. They were all each other had aside from his mother when she was not gallivanting around the world or being pursued by desperate widowers.

"How long will we stay in London, Papa?" Emma looked up at him with dark eyes filled with excitement.

He was happy to see a smile on his daughter's face. If he could do anything for the rest of his life, he would keep Emma happy forever.

"We will stay until..." *Until I am married and no longer obsessing over your governess.* "The end of the season. We shall return before fall." He patted her hand, trying not to follow the trajectory of his thoughts while he was with Emma.

"It's going to be exciting. I get to see grandmother. Miss Beaumont and I will go to Hyde Park and Rotten Row. We'll have ices at Gunter's, go to the museum..." Emma rambled as they reached the small parlor. "Can we go to the dressmakers? I've outgrown all my dresses. Miss Beaumont says I've grown at least three kilometers since she first arrived."

Archie looked at his daughter, laughing, taking his free hand and pressing it to her head as if measuring. "Hmm, I think perhaps one kilometer but surely not three," he teased as they entered the small parlor where Miss Beaumont usually waited for them to join her.

She was always incredibly prompt, a trait he admired most about her. His eyes searched the room, finding her standing by the window, dressed in a pink gown with white satin gloves. Her thick array of curls hung to her shoulders, and he couldn't help but to wonder what they would feel like wrapped around his fingertips. Archie's eyes went to her full decolletage before he wrenched them away to the gold necklace around her neck. He had seen her wear the jewelry often, the flower shape sitting proudly in the valley of her breasts.

"Miss Beaumont, tell Papa I've grown three kilometers not one and a half," Emma demanded of the governess, whose face had lit up at Emma's words.

"Now, Lady Emma, you must remember not to yell." Miss Beaumont sashayed over to them, mesmerizing Archie with the sway of her hips.

"Why? I've heard you yell before, quite often." Emma tilted her head, a trait of her grandmother who did the same thing when she questioned someone.

"Yes, well, I do not wish to marry, but ladies who are in want of a husband do not yell." Miss Beaumont stopped in front of them, tapping Emma's nose affectionately.

He ignored the clenching in his chest from her words. It should not bother him that Miss Beaumont did not want to marry, but in a strange occurrence, it did. It was a shame that no man would never know her passion, feel how soft her skin was, or see the magnificence that lay beneath her clothes.

Archie cleared his throat several times, trying to rid himself of all inappropriate thoughts. "Shall we go into dinner?" he asked, avoiding eye contact with Miss Beaumont.

"Yes, but Miss Beaumont, first tell Papa how much I have grown. He doesn't believe me." Emma raised her face up to her governess.

She wasn't a tall woman, but she was the perfect height for a tall man like himself. Standing in front of him, her head reached slightly above his shoulders, and he could not stop himself from staring. Full lips, long eyelashes, and an aristo-cratic nose that he had not noticed before.

Journey met his gaze, shock registering in her wide-eyed stare, high cheekbones blooming with color before averting her gaze from his. "I assure you, my lord, that Lady Emma has grown significantly in height. I have the markings in the nursery to prove it."

Archie led them all out of the room as Emma bounced happily in front of him and Miss Beaumont. His hand went to the small of Miss Beaumont's back, and the muslin of her gown rubbed against his palm, her body heat searing his skin through the layers of fabric.

A warm feeling of contentment spread throughout his chest, bringing his attention to how domesticated the three of them looked in that moment. They very much resembled a family: a daughter, father, and mother.

He was aware of how absurd the thought was. Not only was Miss Beaumont in his employ, but she was also younger than he was and his daughter's governess.

A governess that Emma loved more than anything in the world.

At that thought, Archie moved his hand away from her person quickly. It felt like he had been burnt by a fire. He needed to remember himself. Miss Beaumont was his employee; that was all.

She could mean nothing else to him.

Chapter Five

After a fulfilling dinner where Lady Emma beguiled Journey and Lord Aberdeen with her ever-increasing French vocabulary, Journey found her nerves increasing with the task at hand. It had taken her days to gather the courage to face the marquess. She had never been a coward, but she found it rather difficult to face him after the events in his study.

The past seven days had been filled with silence and avoidance, but Journey could no longer delay the inevitable. They were leaving for London in three days' time, and as Lady Emma's governess, she was of course expected to travel.

Panic seized her as she sat in the corner of the music room, watching as Lady Emma and Lord Aberdeen played a duet. Journey watched him closely, not only admiring his dark hair and handsome, angular face but his complete love for his daughter. It was hard to ignore what an attentive and dutiful father he was. Although at times he could be maddening, no one could ever doubt his love for his daughter.

"Another," Lady Emma called out once the last note of the piece was done.

"I believe it is Miss Beaumont's turn to entertain us." Lord Aberdeen captured Journey with his heated gaze, and for a single breath of time, she felt wanted.

The evidence of his ardor for her burned in his heated gaze. Journey could see it as his eyes swept down her person before flicking up to pierce her with his need. Journey licked her lips, aware when his eyes darted to hers. She noticed how his pupils dilated, nearly encompassing his sky-blue eyes. It made him appear dangerous to her, and she could feel the effect he was having on her. Clenching her thighs together, Journey's breath caught as she watched Lord Aberdeen stand from the pianoforte.

It was a strange feeling being captured so completely by another person. Journey felt like she had a string connecting her to him, dragging her in slowly.

Lord Aberdeen stopped in front of Journey, offering her his hand. Several moments passed as Journey stared up at him, knowing that once her hand was secure in his, her life could change forever.

She was terrified of change; it took one on a completely different path, and Journey's path was already chosen.

Swallowing, she slowly traced the lines of his hand with her fingertips. She could not ignore the frantic beating of her heart or how heat spread throughout her body from the connection.

Once her hand was in his, he pulled her to her feet, their eyes never moving from each other. She studied his handsome face, realizing that she had never really looked at him. She had spent the past six months trying to ignore him and the attraction she felt. But after the night in his study where she berated him for his unwillingness to fight for enslaved people, she wondered if perhaps she had judged him too harshly. After their disagreement, Journey found books on the abolitionist movement outside her door.

She had poured over the material, wanting to discuss them further with him, but felt that perhaps she did not know his reasons for not continuing the fight. It was difficult to comprehend, especially because she had no choice but to fight.

He was no longer the irate marquess who fought her on every matter concerning his daughter. He was a man who had suffered loss. She could see his pain, felt his sorrow when he spoke of fighting for the ending of the slave trade and his work on the Slave Trade Act of 1807. Journey knew that Lady Emma was born the same year and month that the Slave Trade Act passed, but she did not know why that would stop him from fighting.

Lord Aberdeen stopped in an open space of the music room, jolting Journey back to her surroundings. He stood tall and commanding over her, his wide shoulders strong and straight. She wanted to feel them, to see his bare shoulders. Journey would follow every muscle with her hands, memorizing him so that she could remember him.

"W-what are you doing?" she asked, squinting her eyes at him suspiciously.

The marques positioned her in the center of the room before standing beside her. "I, Miss Beaumont—" The corners of his mouth curved into a smile. "—Am dancing with you."

Lady Emma played the openings to an Allemande. Journey laughed, looking from Lord Aberdeen to his daughter. They both were staring at her with the same twinkle in their eyes.

Journey followed his lead as he began to move, sure and precise. She had only ever danced with her dance instructor, who was strict and firm in his instructions. Her grandmother had wanted to present her to society, but Journey's father would not allow it, and now Journey knew why.

"You tricked me," she told him as she placed her hands on her hip, hopping from foot to foot.

"'Trick' is a strong word. I would say 'coerced.'" He took her arm in his as they danced in a circle.

"Same thing. I was not prepared to entertain tonight, especially in the form of dancing." She was slightly winded from the exertion of dancing, but she couldn't stop the smile that had taken over since the moment they began.

They twirled around each other before they danced closer to the other. Journey felt the connection with each step she took toward him. "Yet for a governess, you're immensely skilled at dancing."

Blinking several times, Journey tried not to show how his words affected her. In the six months in his employ, she had worked to keep some aspects of herself hidden from Lord Aberdeen.

When she first arrived and was questioned about her upbringing and life, Journey left out intimate details to stay hidden from her father's business partner, Mr. Bernard Ramsay. She had been hidden for two years, with the help and assistance of her former governess, Patience Willoughby. Journey had four short months left to stay hidden, and now she was being thrown directly into the fire known as London society.

There would be no hiding from Bernard Ramsay in the middle of Mayfair, and Journey knew that once he found her, she would be forced into a loveless marriage.

Meeting the marquess's eyes, she did every step precisely as she was taught years ago, refusing to pretend in that moment. She was Journey Beaumont, a skilled dancer who had always taken joy in the art. Memories of her time with her grandmother where they would practice the steps that she had been learned filled her mind.

Journey had always loved the Allemande; it was lively and freeing, and she felt a measure of both as she pranced around, not having a care in the world. For a moment she didn't. It was just her and the marquess in their own little corner of the world.

"A governess knows many things, my lord, including dancing." She took his hand as they bounced around, kicking daintily.

She tried to ignore the stroke of his thumb against her skin, how it felt intimate and personal to her. His eyes were full of fire again, causing her once again to question everything that she thought she'd known about the marquess.

"Yes, but you, my Miss Beaumont, are an exceptionally skilled dancer." He released her so that they could dance around each other; however, she could not forget his words.

My Miss Beaumont.

Journey's heart stopped beating, and for a moment she wished she was *his* Miss Beaumont, but she wasn't, and she could not allow him to affect her in such a way. There were many reasons there could never be a relationship between Journey and Lord Aberdeen, but there was only one that mattered to her.

The final chords ended with Journey posing, staring up into the intense gaze of her employer. If it was another lifetime, she knew she would've lost herself to him, but there was no room for love or dashing marquesses in Journey's world.

Lady Emma's loud clapping tore Journey away from Lord Aberdeen as she rose from her pose, watching as Lady Emma ran toward them.

"That was magnificent. I felt like I was at an actual ball." Lady Emma bounced on her slippers, looking from her father to Journey.

"Well, a real ball would actually be crowded and louder. Be happy you won't have to deal with them for some years to come, *fy mach i*." He tapped the tip of Lady Emma's nose, eliciting a giggle from her.

When Journey had first heard the marquess use Welsh

with his daughter, she had ignored the effect it had on her. Hearing the coarse language from his lips made her feel warm inside. There was a softness to him when he spoke the words that Journey learned meant 'my little one.'

"Where did you learn to dance, Miss Beaumont?" Lady Emma asked her as they all stood in the center of the room.

"My grandmother taught me." Journey felt a tug at the side of her mouth at the mention of her grandmother.

She was the one person she could depend on in the world other than her mother, whom she had lost as a girl of eight years. After two years, Journey longed for her grandmother. She had not returned to Heartstone since she learned that Bernard Ramsay was coming to marry her.

Lord Aberdeen's head whipped towards her, his eyes questioning. "Your grandmother? I thought you were an orphan."

Journey looked down, trying not to catch his eye. "I am. My parents died when I was younger, and I stayed with my grandmother for many years when I was a girl."

It wasn't a complete fabrication. She had lived with her grandmother since she was seven, but her parents had still lived. She hated lying to the marquess; however, she wasn't sure that she could trust him with her truth. Four more months, and she could reveal the truth of who she really was.

"My lord, it is time for Lady Emma to retire." Agnes, Lady Emma's maid, walked in, her eyes shifting from Journey to Lord Aberdeen.

"May I please stay just a little while longer?" Lady Emma begged her father, pulling on his arms.

Journey suppressed a laugh, watching the girl's theatrics, while Lord Aberdeen shook his head.

"Time for bed. We'll both see you in the morning. We leave in three days' time." The marquess affectionately tucked a loose strand of hair behind Lady's Emma's ear.

Huffing out in disappointment, Lady Emma mumbled a

reply as she walked out of the music room, closely followed by Agnes, whom Journey saw gave her a reproachful look before leaving.

"Would you like a drink?" the marquess asked, walking over to the sideboard.

Journey tried to find her voice, never one to be shy, but somehow being alone with Lord Aberdeen felt more personal since their time in his study and now the dance. Taking a deep breath, she played with her fingers trying to find the strength to do what was needed of her.

"My lord, I would like to speak to you." Journey held her head high as she walked over to stand beside him.

Lord Aberdeen poured two glasses of port, offering one to Journey, who accepted it readily. She needed something to calm her for what she was going to do. She had to leave Lady Emma earlier than she had expected, but going to London while she was so close to achieving her goal would be foolish.

Journey watched as his shoulders heaved before he cleared his throat and faced her. A shadow of doubt and worry took over his strong features, and she found that she did not care to see him that way. He was a strong man, a loving father, and sometimes a complete horse's ass, but he never doubted himself in her presence.

"Yes, I wanted to speak to you as well." His hand went to her back, guiding her toward the dark-blue sofa. "Shall we sit?"

It was difficult for her to do anything with him so close to her. It was the same feeling that had taken over her earlier before dinner. He overwhelmed her with his presence, his large muscular body encompassing her much smaller one. Journey knew she was safe and secure with him. It was a new feeling for her...security. All her life she had lived with a sense of not belonging anywhere, but from the moment she stepped foot in Plas Castle, she had belonged. Even with their bickering, the marquess had always made her feel safe, like she was a part of something more, a part of a family.

Sitting down, she took a sip of her port before placing it down on the side table. Closing her eyes, she prepared herself for the inevitable. She had to leave Lady Emma—him, she would have to leave him as well.

"Journey?" The sound of her name sounded sensual coming from him. She had never heard him address her by her given name, and now that she had, Journey did not know if she ever wanted him to call her "Miss Beaumont" again.

A touch to her cheek had her eyes flying open, and there he was in front of her, his eyes filled with concern. "Are you well?"

Nodding, she placed her hand over his, their fingers intertwining on her cheek. She could feel his breath on her lips, see every detail in his sky-blue eyes. Journey could lose herself in his gaze, and dear God, did she want to. She was tired of ignoring the palpable attraction that she felt for him.

Placing their joined hands in her lap, she tried to free him from her hold, but he gripped her hand tighter.

Finding her strength, she pressed on, her mouth dry. "Lord Aberdeen—"

"'Archie.' Please call me 'Archie.'" He squeezed her hand, their connection and his proximity causing her to forget herself.

It would be so easy to allow him access into her life...her heart.

No.

She couldn't call him by his given name and dance with him and sit next to him as if they were a courting couple and not an employee and employer.

Journey stood, desperate for space, her hand going to her abdomen, trying to control the wave of emotions that spun inside of her like a hurricane. It was destroying every wall she had ever built around herself to protect her from everyone that wanted something from her.

She felt him behind her before he spoke a single word. His heat and scent overwhelmed her, and she wanted to fall back into his arms. "Journey, I don't mean to keep offending you. I'm finding it rather difficult to control myself around you."

His confession shocked her, only because she too was having trouble controlling herself around him. Since the moment they met, there was an attraction that she had tried to ignore, but it was forever present whenever he was near.

Releasing the breath she was holding, she faced him, ready to stand firm in her decision. "Lord Aberdeen...I regret to inform you that I cannot travel to London with you and Lady Em...Emma." Her voice broke at the thought of leaving the little girl who had become an instant part of Journey's life. "I am submitting my resignation."

"If it's because of what's happening between us, I assure you I will be the perfect gentleman." He took a step forward, closing the gap between them. "Please stay with us, Journey."

She shook her head, trying to control the onslaught of emotions that was washing over her. "There is nothing between us. I am your employee. That is all."

He took another step forward. "I keep telling myself that, too." His eyes captured hers; his lips parted as though he was winded from his confession. "You were right when you said I stopped fighting, but I want to fight." Another step had him so close that all she had to do was lean forward and press her lips to his. "I want to fight for this feeling that has consumed me for six long, agonizing months." His hand wrapped around her waist, pulling her flush against him. "I want to fight for you."

Journey could take no more, and for the first time in her

life, she did something without thinking of all of her responsibilities and the people who depended on her. She thought only of him and her in that moment when she pressed her lips to his.

Chapter Six

Archie was finding it difficult to recall his own name. The Houses of Parliament escaped him, and he wasn't sure if he was in England or Wales. In truth, the only thing that he could comprehend was that his lips were finally on hers. She was kissing him. Journey, not Miss Beaumont.

Her Christian name had slipped out of his mouth without his permission, and now he wanted to say it always. Archie wanted to whisper her name in the middle of the night while she was wrapped in his arms.

Tightening his grip around her waist, his free hand went to the nape of her neck as he controlled her movements. He dominated the kiss, his tongue slowly caressing her full bottom lip, begging for permission. Her whimpered sigh was all he needed as she opened to him.

The first taste nearly caused his legs to buckle. She was sweeter than he had imagined. Her innocence was evident in her shy, hesitant kisses. The Miss Beaumont he knew did not have a shy or hesitant quality in her.

Her hand running through his shoulder-length hair sent

desire running through him as he backed her against the wall. For a moment, they did nothing but kiss. She had completely overwhelmed him in the six months she had lived at Plas Castle. Archie was done trying to control himself. He had warred with himself for months.

No more waiting and denying himself of the sweet pleasure of her.

Journey.

Archie's fingertips caressed the curls at the nape of her neck. They were softer than he had envisioned, tickling his fingers and his hands while he plundered her mouth. Pulling her head back slightly, he deepened the kiss, feeling warmth throughout his body.

His hard cock reminded him that it had been years since he was with a woman. However, she wasn't just anyone. He knew how passionate she was; he knew she loved his daughter so much that she had tolerated his irate behavior for months.

Archie knew he would never tire of kissing her.

Trailing fevered kisses from her lips to the column of her neck, he licked and sucked, reveling in the sounds she was making. Her whimpers and gasps of pleasure sent chills tingling down his spine, and he wanted every breath of hers. Archie's free hand roamed the curves of her body through the muslin gown, and dear God, he was going to explode.

When Journey's neck fell back, Archie seized the opportunity to suck gently at her pulse point, his hand finding a permanent home on her rounded backside. He let out an animalistic groan, wishing he could feel her skin without the impediment of clothing in his way.

"Archie," she whispered.

The breathy sound of his name fueled him as he pressed himself against her arching body.

He shook as he tried to restrain himself because he knew

he couldn't claim her in the music room. She deserved better, and he wanted to give her everything.

Releasing his hold on her person, he buried his head in the sweet confines of her neck, inhaling her scent as he tried to bring his lust under control. Archie couldn't remember when he was affected in such a way by a woman. Not even his late wife awakened the passion that Journey elicited from him.

A slight nudge of his shoulders brought him back from the lust-fueled haze that had taken over him.

Looking up into light-brown eyes, he saw hesitation in her gaze. Pressing a soft kiss to her swollen lips, he stood looking down at her. "What is it, *fy nghariad aur*?" he asked, stroking a finger down her soft cheek.

She blinked up at him, confused by his Welsh. His father had spoken Welsh all of Archie's life, and he wanted his own children to speak it and have it a part of their everyday life. "What did you say?" she asked.

He kissed the tip of her long nose. "I said, 'What is it, my golden darling?'"

She stared at him for a moment before color stained her cheeks from his term of endearment. "We can't do this. I'm your daughter's governess and in your employ." She pushed him further away, standing from the wall.

"Will you deny what is between us?" he asked, watching as she ran her hand through her curls.

His hands twitched with the need to feel each curly brown tress wrapped around his fingers again.

"Y-yes." Her voice broke, and he watched as her bottom lip quivered. It was then he knew that she wanted him as much as he wanted her. "We've denied ourselves for six months. Nothing has changed."

"Everything has changed." He pulled her towards him, her pliable body coming willingly. "Your taste is forever branded in my soul."

His lips captured hers, tasting and teasing. Now that he'd had the pleasure of feeling her against his body, he didn't think he could ever let her go.

Ending the kiss, she dropped her head, resting it against Archie's chin. He kissed the top of her head, chuckling. For the first time in years, he felt happy. Archie had known happiness since Katherine died, but it was always associated with Emma. What he was feeling in that moment was a joy at finding the one person who was perfect for him.

When he was young, he fell in love with Katherine, and they were impulsive and reckless. Now he was older and wiser and had Emma to consider with every decision he made. Yet Archie felt ill-prepared for the emotions he was feeling for his daughter's governess.

Journey took a step back, her light eyes watering. He reached for her, but she refused, walking away from him. Archie felt empty without her near. It was a funny feeling—now that he'd had her, he always wanted her with him.

Archie watched as she went to the sofa, picking up her long-forgotten port and taking a hearty sip. Following, he sat beside her, wanting to be patient and give her the time she needed.

"I can't go to London. I was giving you my resignation as Emma's governess." She took another sip of her port, avoiding eye contact with him.

He knew that there was something she wasn't telling him. Since the moment she had arrived, he knew that Journey Beaumont had a secret.

"Why can't you travel to London, Journey?" He took her free hand in his, stroking her long, elegant fingers.

He watched as she swallowed, nervously looking around the piano room. He had always loved the room that was filled with multiple instruments. He and his parents had all been music lovers, and now Emma loved it as well.

Releasing a deep sigh, Journey looked up at him, his golden darling. "I don't want to lie to you, Archie, but I can't risk being discovered in London."

Wrapping his arm around her waist, he cupped her cheek, wanting her to know exactly how he felt about her. "You can trust me, *fy nghariad aur*. I wish you knew that."

He felt her shiver at his words and wondered what he said that had affected her. He watched as she licked her lips, her gaze becoming heated as if he had said something sensual.

She chuckled at him, giving him a breathtaking smile. "It should be a sin for you to speak Welsh."

"*Yn wir?*" he asked, winking at her.

"Now you're just being cruel," she told him, watching the fire in his eyes.

Leaning closer, his grip tightened around her waist while his free hand traveled up her glove-covered hand. "Do you like when I speak Welsh?" he whispered, skimming her cheek with his lips.

She licked her lips, drawing his attention to the plump flesh. "Yes."

His lips continued tracing a path to her ear as he licked the shell before taking her earlobe into his mouth. She let out a hum of contentment, the sound traveling directly to his hard member.

"I want you to be honest with yourself, *fy nghariad aur*. Do you want to leave us?" he asked, taking her by the chin and turning her toward him.

"No."

He watched her, seeing the honesty in her eyes. "Good." He kissed her lips sweetly before sitting back against the sofa, taking her with him.

Pulling her closer to him, he rested his head on top of her head, kissing her wild curls. "There will be no more talk of leaving, but when you're ready, I want you to tell me what you're afraid of, and we'll face it together."

She lifted her face toward his, pulling him down to place a kiss on his lips. "Thank you, Archie. I will tell you when I'm ready."

Archie pressed his head against hers, looking into her eyes. He knew the truth of his heart; he always had. Even as a young man of eight and ten, he knew what he wanted. Now that he was older, he was even more confident of his choices and his heart.

Journey Beaumont would be his, and no title, rank, or society would stand in his way.

Chapter Seven

F our days later, Journey found herself being jostled in a carriage as they traveled to London. They had left Plas Castle before the sun had risen in the sky. The eerie darkness reminded her of life on the plantation. She would often be awakened to the enslaved men and women of the plantation starting their day well before the sun rose. Journey remembered running down in nothing but her nightclothes to play with her cousins, but none of them could play with her then because they had to work on the sugar cane farm. There was no choice for them, no warm bed, no home. They weren't free like Journey, yet they were still her family.

The trip from the castle through North Wales was filled with Lady Emma talking incessantly even with Journey giving her several tasks to do. The girl was swift in her reading, diligent in mathematics, and becoming fluent in French. When Journey ran out of material for the highly intelligent child, she began questioning her on the towns they were passing, the Snowdonia Mountains, and a complete history on the royal family.

Journey was pleased when Lady Emma started nodding

off as they began reading about Henry VIII and his many wives. She loved the little girl, but being stuck in a carriage with her insistent chattering in addition to her father's heated gazes made Journey wish for a moment of peace if only for her to think clearly.

Looking down at the sleeping girl with her head rested in her lap, Journey felt a small smile grace her lips. Across from them Lord Aberdeen, *Archie*, sat reading, looking devastatingly handsome and distinguished. Although...she still wasn't accustomed to calling him by his Christian name or receiving attentions from him. After their first night in the music room, they had spent every night after dinner together once Lady Emma had retired.

Journey never missed the looks of distain that Agnes gave her when she would leave Journey alone in the music room with Archie. She had noticed some of the servants whispering but had heard nothing from her friend, Henrietta, who she had grown close to over her months at Plas.

She was aware of what it looked like. She had never stayed behind with Archie before, always choosing to retire when Lady Emma was done for the night. Like him, she too had denied their attraction for one another and was tired of running from it.

Archie placed his book on the pristine leather seat beside him. "Perhaps you should straighten her neck. I'd hate for her to wake in pain."

Journey did everything in her power to not roll her eyes at his comment. After all, her grandmother had always reminded her that it was not ladylike. "She's fine, Archie." She gritted out, trying to reassure him.

"Is she sound asleep?" He reached out his hand for hers, and she placed her bare hand in his.

She had long abandoned her gloves, finding them a hindrance while they were traveling. It all felt very domestic, reaching a part of her heart she did not know existed. Journey had given up on all dreams of a family. Now she wondered if she was denying herself happiness by prioritizing others' lives over hers.

Ignoring her thoughts, Journey moved the dark mass of hair aside to reveal Lady Emma's sleeping face. "She is. I believe Lady Emma is a very sound sleeper. Once I came into her room to retrieve some books and dropped them loud on the floor, and she did not stir at all."

Archie chuckled, looking over at his sleeping daughter. "Yes, she inherited that particular trait from her mother."

At the mention of his late wife, she watched him closely, seeing warmth take over him. In her stay at Plas, she had not heard much of the late marchioness. All she knew was that Lady Aberdeen was very young when she died in childbirth. She had heard tales of their love when she first arrived. It all made Journey wonder what was she doing with him.

"What was she like, your late wife?" she asked as he stroked her fingertips.

He smiled before he answered her. "Katherine was wild and hated the rules of society. She broke them every chance she could."

"Sounds like I would've liked her," Journey told him, watching how his eyes crinkled at the corners.

Archie sat forward, enveloping her hand in both of his. He had surprised her with just how affectionate he was with her. He kissed Journey's wrist, the simple act causing her heart to beat rapidly in her chest. "You would have, and she would've liked you as well. She admired any woman who was able to provide for herself in our world."

"Did she assist you with the Slave Trade Act?" Journey asked, enjoying learning about the woman who had given her life for her child.

It made her think of her own mother and the last time that

she saw her alive and happy. Journey was a little younger than Lady Emma when she last saw her mother. They had been on the porch of the home Journey had lived in all her life, and she had not known why her Papa was sending her away with her grandmother. If she closed her eyes, she could still smell her mother, could feel her arms around her as they said goodbye. Journey could hear the whispered words still. *"Always remember who you are and where you've come from."*

Archie released her hand, sitting back against the leather of the seat. His face had drained of color, his pale skin looking nearly white. Journey searched her mind trying to figure out what it was that she had said that made him look so stricken.

"No." He picked up his book as if the subject was closed.

"You wish me to open up about my life, yet you refuse to do the same." Her hands shook as she tried to fight the onslaught of emotions that tried to bombard her. She had believed that he really did have feelings for her, so much so that he gave her the choice to tell him about her own demons when she was ready. Yet he would not share his own.

Journey's blood ran cold in her veins, her abdomen swirled, and she thought she was going to be sick with the constant of swaying of the carriage. She cursed herself for being weak enough to let him in when he would not do the same.

"That's different. I want to know more about you." He raked his hand through his shoulder-length hair in frustration. "I know you're hiding something from me. I've known ever since you arrived."

She swung her gaze toward him. "What does it matter if you're not willing to share your own secrets, Lord Aberdeen?"

She watched him struggle with words, his mouth opening and closing like a fish out of the sea. A sigh of relief escaped her moments later when the carriage stopped. Night had fallen, the moonlight casting an eerie glow from the sky, and she was in desperate need of sleep. There was no time to dwell on her own weakness. It was her decision to kiss Lord Aberdeen, hers and hers alone. Now she knew how he really felt about her.

Archie exited the carriage first as Journey woke Lady Emma from her sound resting place on her lap. She watched as the little girl stretched like a cat, letting out a loud yawn. Journey was going to miss the small girl with a big personality. The door to the carriage opened, letting the cool night air in.

"The marquess went to secure rooms for the night, Miss Beaumont." The coachman, Thomas, watched her closely from the door. Journey ignored his lingering gaze, deciding to focus on Lady Emma who was currently blinking as she looked around the carriage.

"Thank you, Thomas. Please shut the door before Lady Emma catches a chill." He nodded before closing the door.

Journey let out a sigh of relief. She did not want to be rude to Thomas who upon her arrival had tried to show interest in her. Not only was she not interested in the blond-haired, blue-eyed coachman, but since the moment she had arrived, she'd fought the attraction she felt for Lord Aberdeen.

Until they were alone in the music room.

"Where is Papa?" Lady Emma asked, her head craning to see outside the small carriage window.

Journey smiled fondly at the girl with her wild mane of unruly black hair and sleep-heavy eyes. She tried in vain to make Lady Emma presentable to be seen in public, but she knew the girl's hair was unmanageable with its thick curls.

Lady Emma hugged her body close to Journey's, laying her head under her chin. Journey tried to fight the onslaught of emotion that was taking over her. In six short months, the girl had captured Journey's heart completely.

Her fingers stopped combing through the thick mass of black curls, her eyes watering slightly at how comfortable Lady

Emma was with her. Closing her eyes, she fought away the tears. She always knew that she was going to leave Emma. Plas Castle wasn't her home; she did not belong there. Perhaps she did not belong anywhere.

The door of the carriage opened, revealing a red-cheeked marquess, the cold Welsh weather attacking him furiously. Journey watched as his eyes softened at the sight of her and Lady Emma before he cleared his throat. "The rooms are ready. I've arranged for meals to be sent up."

"Papa, I'm tired." She released Journey before she flung herself at her father.

He lifted her out of the carriage, not caring for propriety, and once again, Journey's heart softened toward this man who loved his daughter more than anything else in the world. He reached for her with the hand that was not securing Lady Emma. She looked at it skeptically, deciding that she needed to end things.

It had gone too far. She had forgotten herself but not again. Her purpose was clear: she could not be distracted by Archibald Huxley no matter how much he loved his daughter.

Stepping out the carriage without his assistance, Journey ignored the feel of him beside her. Archie's hand took her by the elbow leading her toward the inn while the other servants walked in a different direction.

"Lord Aberdeen?" Journey inquired, wondering why she was not going to the servants' quarters.

"I have gotten you rooms in the inn, Miss Beaumont," Lord Aberdeen's voice was curt as he guided her toward the door of the inn before stopping. "Agnes, please see to Lady Emma. I'm afraid she is rather exhausted."

"Of course, my lord," Agnes replied before she followed them into the establishment.

In her twenty years of living, Journey was accustomed to silencing rooms when she entered. Either because of her color or because of her station, she never cared to know. There were hundreds of thousands of people of African descent free across the world, yet somehow people were still shocked when she entered a room. Perhaps it was the quality of her clothes that had been made by one of the finest dressmakers in England. Journey had taken her most worn-down dresses, but even those were finer than most people had ever seen.

"This way, my lord." The innkeeper let them up the stairs where the rooms were located. He waved to three rooms. "The best for you and your family, Lord Aberdeen."

"Thank you. Please have dinner sent up," Archie called to the innkeeper who was openly staring at Journey.

"O-of course, my lord," he answered, his eyes going to Archie's hold on Journey's elbow.

Journey held her tongue as she walked into the first room where Archie laid a sleeping Lady Emma down on the brass bed. The room was luxurious compared to the ones Journey stayed in on her way to Plas Castle. The fire burned high, heating the entire room. It was clean, the bed covered in a thick duvet; a picture of the Prince Regent sat above the bed.

Journey could hear the wind blowing outside, rattling against the windowsill.

Journey assisted Agnes with removing Lady Emma's cape coat, the thick wool protecting the girl from the cold. She chuckled, watching Lady Emma's limp body sway to the side.

"She sleeps like the dead," Agnes commented looking at Lady Emma.

"She does indeed. Do you need me to assist you with her?" Journey asked, noticing that Lord Aberdeen was outside the door speaking with the innkeeper.

"No, I have her Miss Beaumont." Agnes pierced Journey with older, wiser eyes. She wasn't more than ten years Journey's senior, but she felt much older than Journey's twenty years. A soft hand gripped hers. "Be careful. Great men never marry their servants."

She had no words to that bit of wisdom because she knew it was true, but what did it matter? Journey was leaving in four months.

There was no other choice.

Chapter Eight

S hadows from the fire danced around the large and inviting room as Archie sat staring into its red and orange embers. He had long removed his tailcoat, waistcoat, and cravat to free himself of the constrains that were choking him. Finally, his past had caught up with his future, and he was at a loss as to what to do about it.

He had never thought that he would want another woman after Katherine's death. Archie thought there was no chance that he was meant find happiness not once but twice. He had given up all hope of finding a person to spend the rest of his life with. Emma was his sole priority, his reason for living. Until six months prior when Journey Beaumont sashayed into his study, tearing his world apart.

He took a drink of the brandy he procured from the innkeeper, letting the rich liquid soothe him. He needed to speak to Journey, but what was he going to say? That he had failed Katherine because of his obsession with justice and freedom?

Finishing his drink, Archie tried to find the courage to

share his greatest failure with her. Their disagreement in the carriage left him unsettled. He wanted nothing more than to tell her everything about himself, but he was afraid of what she would think when she finally learned the truth.

Sighing in frustration, he rose to his feet, tired of hiding like a small child. Archie did not think as he walked out of his room to hers. The hour was late, but he needed her to know everything.

Knocking on her door, he stood in the dark hall lit by candelabras. All was quiet, the entire inn abed for the night.

"Who is it?" Her deep sultry voiced greeted him from the other side of the door.

"Aberdeen." He could hear the pounding of his heart in his ears. Archie was afraid for the first time in nine years.

The door opened slowly. Journey peeped from behind it to ensure it was really him. She opened the door wider, and Archie walked into the room.

He watched as Journey closed the door, turning to lean against it. Her hair was braided in sections, making her appear younger. She was wearing nothing but a chemise and a shawl. His greedy mind wanted to see her uncovered before him.

"You shouldn't have come. It's the middle of the night, and you're my employer and nothing else." The last part of her sentence was said with finality, breaking him into pieces.

"I need to speak to you. It could not wait until morning." He took a step toward her, wanting to wrap her in his arms, but was halted by her raised hand.

"You may speak, but I cannot assure you I will listen." Her coldness was expected but still a shock to his system.

Looking around her room, he noted it was as large as his with a chaise lounge. The oversized bed sat against the wall, increasing his nerves.

Archie walked over to the chaise, sitting down with his

hands clasped together. He knew if he wanted more with Journey that he would have to be honest with her. Though she still had not confessed all of her secrets to him, he knew that it was difficult for her to trust.

Katherine never had anything to do with the abolitionist's movement, especially with her older brother's ties to slavery. No, it was Archie who had given everything for the cause, and it cost him greatly.

"When I met Katherine, I had already inherited the title and assumed my seat in Parliament." Archie couldn't look at Journey, so he fixed his eyes on a particular part of the dull brown carpet that was lighter than the entire room. "Before I joined Parliament, I was very much involved in the abolitionist movement, and when I took my seat, it was as if I had a stage for my cause."

Journey sat down at the foot of the bed, careful to keep her distance from Archie. He wanted her closer to him, if only just to feel her warmth as he bared his soul to her.

He continued, licking his dry lips and trying to find courage. After all these years, he still felt responsible for Katherine's death. "I fought tirelessly to end the Slave Trade Act. It was my one goal, and nothing else mattered to me until I met Katherine. We were a love match, yet I never stopped fighting for the ending of the slave trade."

"Did Katherine join the movement with you?" Journey's intense gaze pierced him. Her shawl had fallen off her shoulders, taking the sleeve of her chemise with it, revealing creamy brown skin.

She covered herself once she noticed him staring at her bare shoulder. Archie wanted to see all of her. He knew she thought he was indifferent and uncaring, but he was never a man for dalliances. Archie wanted her, and in his mind, that was forever.

"No. Although she did not agree with the slave trade, she

never openly fought against it since her father's second-eldest son was very much involved in slavery." Archie watched as Journey blanched, color draining from her brown skin. "Do not think ill of Katherine."

She shook her head, her eyes glazing over with secrets. He wanted to know them all but knew she still was not ready. "I do not judge her. Sometimes we cannot help who we are related to."

He wanted to press the subject more, but tonight was about his truths. They would have time for hers.

"Katherine and I had an instant connection...we were married, and less than two years later, she was with child... Emma." He smiled fondly at the memory of discovering they were expecting. "I never stopped fighting for the cause. In fact I fought even harder, hoping that my child would be born into a world without slavery."

He paused, allowing the silence to strengthen him. It was hard for him to continue; he had never spoken of it to a single person. Not Richmore or even Archie's own mother knew his part in Katherine's death. He had replayed the events of those months over in his mind for the past nine years, wishing that he had returned home sooner...if only to say goodbye.

"We were so close to the bill passing. I-I left Katherine months before her confinement. I wrote to her at every opportunity, but I never returned to Plas." He couldn't continue, the words choking him, his heart beating uncontrollably. He felt as if he was reliving that time of his life all over again. Covering his face with his hands, Archie rubbed at his tired eyes. If only he hadn't been so invested, perhaps Emma would still have a mother.

He felt soft hands run through his hair. Looking up at Journey, he was rendered speechless by her beauty and the care in her eyes. "What happened?"

"I received a letter from Katherine nearly two months

earlier, informing me that the doctor thought the babe would come soon and that she wanted me home." He shook his head, remembering every detail as if it happened yesterday. "Our mothers were with her, so I foolishly thought that I could stay until the bill passed. We were so close I couldn't leave it, thinking it was the most important work that I would ever do."

Journey knelt in front of him, placing her hand on his cheek. He leaned into her touch, craving her strength to soothe him. "I knew the bill was going to pass. All I had to do was stay in town just a little longer. It passed, and Richmore and I celebrated, delaying my return by a day or two." He swallowed the lump in his throat, knowing if he stopped now, he would never be strong enough to admit the truth. "When I arrived at the castle to find my wife and newborn child...my mother greeted me at the door with Emma in her arms and tears in her eyes."

"Oh, Archie, I'm so sorry, but you must know that was not your fault." She lifted his head so that they could meet eye to eye. "You fought for what is right, for what every person should have, freedom. You fought for freedom, but that did not cause Katherine's death, and giving up won't bring her back."

He wrapped his arms around her waist, pulling her to him so that he could rest his head against her abdomen. Her spicy scent engulfed him, and he buried his nose in the cotton of her chemise, wanting to bask in it. His eyes closed automatically as she stroked his hair.

Moments passed as he gathered his thoughts, allowing his breathing to regain a steady pace before he raised his head. Archie looked at her, seeing understanding in her light-brown gaze. It was not at all what he expected. He thought she would run away from him after learning the truth. "Now you know why I can't fight—"

"You can fight, Archie. People still need you to fight. *My* family needs you!" Journey stood, marching away as emotions took hold of her.

For a moment Archie wished he misunderstood her, but he saw her honesty and knew that she had family still in bondage. Hundreds of questions ran though his mind. Was she ever enslaved? *Dear God, no.*

He followed after her, wrapping his arms around her waist, pulling her back flush to his chest. He held her like that, the shivers coming from her body, breaking his heart.

"Who?" he asked, kissing the top of her head, wanting to allow her a semblance of comfort. But how could he comfort her from such atrocities in the world?

He waited patiently for her answer, his hold tightening as he listened to her cry. Archie wanted to carry her pain away, but he could not imagine the horrors she had seen or gone through. Archie had seen many depictions of slavery, heard horror stories through his work with the abolitionist's movements.

"My mother's siblings and their children." She took a deep breath, the movement moving them both up and down. "They all are enslaved back home in Jamacia where I was born."

"*Fy nghariad aur,*" he whispered, turning her to face him. Archie needed to see her, to let her know that she was not alone, and he would do everything in his power to help her.

Wiping her tears away, he held her face, staring into her golden eyes. From the moment he first saw her, they had captured him completely, rendering him speechless.

Journey took his hand in hers, closing her fingers around his. He felt whole and complete. It was a feeling that he had never felt before, and it scared him.

She looked up at him with watery eyes. "That is why you can't give up. Because of people like my family who are still in bondage." She swallowed holding his gaze. "I need you to fight."

Chapter Nine

Journey laid beside Archie in the large bed, her fingertips playing with the hairs on his chest. She had been fascinated with the opening of his shirt sleeves since he walked into her room, now she could not stop touching him as they laid on top of the duvet talking. The only person she had ever spoken too in great lengths about any subject was her grandmother.

She also confided in her former governess, who had been like an elder sister to her, as well as Henrietta who she met at Plas. Speaking with Archie felt more intimate in so many ways, perhaps because they were in bed holding each other.

It was the most natural thing in the world to lay in his arms and talk about her family. To listen to tales about Katherine, his mother, Richmore, and Lady Emma.

"How did your mother become free and not her siblings?" Archie stroked her bare shoulder, innocently sending fire swirling through her.

Being so intimate with a man was a new experience for her. Nevertheless, she couldn't stop touching him or kissing any part of his exposed flesh. He had bared a part of his soul to her, confessing his failure to put his family first over the cause.

Journey understood him more than he knew. She had spent her life waiting to come of age so that she would be able to return to Jamaica and free every slave at the plantation. Then she would live the rest of her life fighting for freedom, making the old plantation a working one where the enslaved were free and earned wages. If they chose to leave after she freed them all, that was perfectly fine with Journey.

"My father fell in love with her, so much so that he freed her." She sighed, remembering the story from when she was younger. Her mother had recited the events of her and Journey's father's romance. Journey had been younger than Lady Emma at the time, and even then, the story did not sit well with her.

Archie sat up slightly, the cotton of his shirt sleeve rubbing against her cheek. "Is your father an Englishman?"

"Yes, and like all English gentlemen, he sent me to England when I was very young to be raised by my grandmother." A small smile graced Journey's lips at the thought of her grandmother.

The Countess of Wiltmore was a formidable force even at the ripe age of seventy. She often reminded Journey that she would outlive everyone. Despite her growing age the countess was healthy and thriving.

"Both of your parents perished?" Archie's whispered words pierced her heart.

She had lost her mother years earlier, yet she remembered reading the letter from her father. It was surprisingly cold, informing her that her mother had died. "Yes. M-my mother when I was nine." It was still difficult to speak of seventeen years later. Her mother had been the center of her entire world until her father had arranged for Journey to be educated with her grandmother. "I wrote to her every day for nearly two years. She would write me back. She taught herself how to read and write and oversaw my education until I left."

The tears fell freely as they always did anytime she spoke of her mother. Remembering her was painful.

"She sounds like a magnificent woman who raised a magnificent woman." Archie wrapped one of her long sleeping braids around his finger. "Why didn't your father free her siblings and their families?"

"I do not know; all I know is that I will free every last one of them one day. I won't stop until there aren't any enslaved men or women at White Rose Plantation." Journey closed her eyes, feeling the hour and the weight of their conversation take hold of her.

She was exhausted from running and lying for months. All she wanted to do was sleep in his arms and forget everything if only for a moment.

Journey's body relaxed, sleep taking over her. She knew that she needed to tell Archie about her leaving England, her inheritance, and Ramsay, but she could not do anything but allow the peaceful bliss to take over her.

～

JOURNEY AWOKE TO STRONG, warm arms wrapped around her. It felt as if she was basking in the Jamaican sun, and she wanted to stay there forever. She breathed deeply. Inhaling she took in sandalwood and male, her eyes flying open to reveal that she was tucked securely in Archie's arms. Her head was positioned under his chin, her face lying in the opening of his shirt sleeve as her body practically laid on top of his.

Her hand came up to check if she'd slept in her head scarf. She had not, and she cursed herself for forgetting, knowing that her hair would be frizzy for the remainder of the day.

Raising her head she noted that they fell asleep on top of the embroidered duvet.

A kiss to the top of her head alerted Journey that she was not the only one awake at that ungodly hour. Once again, she had risen before the sun, but unlike the previous night where she woke alone, this time she awoke in heaven. Pure and complete heaven.

A soft kiss to her forehead awakened her body, heat swirling in her abdomen. Raising herself up, Journey offered him her lips, desperate to feel his against hers. He claimed them hungrily, taking her top lip into his mouth and sucking lightly. Wrapping her arms around his neck, Journey grabbed at his thick dark tresses as she slid her body fully on top of his.

His large hands roamed her body, pulling her chemise further up with every purposeful caress. She couldn't control the whimpers that escaped her when his bare hand met her overheated flesh. Deepening the kiss, Journey pressed her needy core against the hardness in his breeches, seeking and searching for relief to quench the overwhelming need pulsing through her.

Journey's own hand found the sinewy flesh under his shirt sleeve, his groan of enjoyment sending power coursing through her. Exploring the muscles of his chest, she could feel the rapid beating of his heart as her hand explored, her finger-tips grazing over his hard nipple, eliciting a wanton moan from deep in his throat.

She was tired of running, exhausted from all the lies she had been told her entire life, from the ones she still had to tell every day. In a world filled with lies, he was the one thing that was solely true and honest.

Archie.

He made her feel alive in ways she had never imagined, and she couldn't walk away from that single unquenchable feeling without drinking.

With her mind settled, Journey gave him one last searing kiss, taking his bottom lip between her teeth. She let out a yelp of surprise as his strong body surged forward, his member rubbing gloriously against a particularly pleasing spot that sent jolts of intense pleasure scoring through her.

"Archie," she moaned, his name coming out as a prayer.

Sitting up, Journey pulled the thin chemise over her head, revealing all of herself to him. She watched Archie's breath come out in heavy pants as one of his hands trailed up her flat abdomen. She watched him closely as she licked her swollen, kissed lips. They still tingled and ached from their kisses. She wanted more of him, to feel the pressure and intensity of their kiss...forever.

She ignored the frazzled nerves that tried to take hold of her. This was her decision, and she chose him, wanted more of his hands on her. Journey needed to feel him everywhere, and she would not let anything deter her from having him. It was only her and Archie in that moment and no one else. No past, no pain, just them.

"Christ, *cariad*, I won't be able to control myself," he gritted out the words, as one hand cupped her full breast, the other squeezing her round bottom.

She wanted to ask him the meaning of *cariad,* but she couldn't think or form a coherent thought. Journey was needy, and only he could satisfy her. "I don't want your control." She leaned over, kissing him slow, her tongue dipping, tasting, savoring every part of him.

No, she wanted him to lose control...and he did.

Archie flipped her over, taking control of the kiss. One of his hands pulled at the hair that had come undone from her nightly braids. He dominated her every move, his large body pressing into hers, hands traveling all over her body. Journey loved every second of it, and she craved more.

Her hands pulled at his shirt sleeve, needing to feel his skin against hers. Ending their desperate kiss, Archie wrenched the garment over his head, throwing it across the room.

Journey watched as he rose from the bed. She immediately felt cold and alone. Her eyes followed his movements as he tore his breeches open. "Get under the duvet," he ordered.

She followed his command, crawling under the duvet and sheets. The cool cotton rubbed against her bare nipples, and she squeezed her legs together, trying to control the ache in her core. Journey turned to face Archie, watching as his tall, wide, muscular body climbed into bed with her.

A dark thatch of hair covered his firm chest, leading the path to a perfect abdomen. Journey had a brief glimpse of his long, thick manhood before his body disappeared under the covers.

Disappointment washed over her at not being allowed to see all of him fully, a pout forming on her lips until Archie claimed them in his. He kissed her furiously, savoring her, his strong hands around her neck as he pulled her to him. Her body was pliant and willing under his control.

Sounds of the inn waking filled the room, but Journey did not care.

The feel of his naked body against hers did nothing to quench her need for him. Her abdomen was in knots, her heart beating wildly as their hands explored each other. Archie kissed her neck, his hand traveling up the apex of her thighs to the thatch of hair between her legs.

Holding her breath, she kissed the top of his head, inhaling his scent. She gripped his shoulders as he teased her sensitive flesh with his fingers.

"You're so wet for me, *fy nghariad aur*," he murmured against her overheated skin as he took a dark-brown nipple into his warm mouth.

Journey arched up into him, his fingertips teasing the small nub of her sex. She was assaulted with an onslaught of emotions, her body tensing, something building inside of her like a rising tide.

Archie dipped a finger inside of her heated core, causing Journey to gasp. Sighing, she could feel her muscles clench as he added a second finger. She felt full, as he moved in and out of her, the feel of his mouth teasing and sucking on her sensitive nipple all caused her body to shiver and coil until she burst.

Her eyes squeezed shut as she arched up to meet his hand, needing more. Her feet dug into the thin mattress as she thrusted up toward him, her body begging for more. Journey cried out in bliss as Archie moved to her other breast, biting and sucking as he did the other nipple. His fingers never stopped moving inside of her, and she rode out her pleasure, her fingers digging into his shoulders.

"Archie." Taking hold of his hair, she pulled him to her, crashing her mouth to his, tasting, savoring. "I need you."

"I need to taste you first, *cariad*, and then I am all yours." He kissed her one last time before he licked a sensual trail from her lips down the center of her body, stopping to lick her navel.

She couldn't stop the needy whimpers nor did she comprehend what he meant by *tasting her*. Until he continued his path to her sex that was still sensitive from his attentions.

Lifting on her elbows, Journey watched as Archie reached her core, his hungry dark eyes holding her gaze as he licked up her center. She couldn't breathe, the exotic sight of him rendered her speechless, and she questioned if she hadn't somehow died.

"Watch me," he commanded her, and she had no choice but to obey.

Journey couldn't deny him if she wanted to. The sight of him between her parted thighs excited her so much that she quivered all over. She watched wide eyed as he took a deep inhale of her scent, groaning as if it was the most decadent thing he had ever experienced.

A slow kiss to her sex lit a fire in her that traveled from her toes to her rapidly beating heart. She had no opportunity to prepare herself as he began licking her, first slowly, tentatively, and then he was feasting on her.

One of his arms laid across her middle, cementing her in place. Journey fell back against the array of pillows unable to contain herself any longer. Her hands pulled at his hair, finding the exquisite torture so divine that she never wanted him to stop. She tried to contain her cries of passion, but she could not restrain herself. The feelings were so overwhelming that she thought her heart would expire.

The familiar bliss from moments ago swirled in her abdomen as Archie focused all his attentions to the bundle of nerves at her sex. Journey cried out in pure ecstasy when he added two fingers, dipping and exploring her. One single hook on his fingers had her entire body soaring into the heavenly abyss of pleasure.

She pulled on his hair, trying to stop his relentless pursuit but he would not.

"Archie, I-I cannot bear anymore. It's too much!" She cried out as another wave washed over her, her body shaking, her hips swerving toward him, her greedy body begging for more while her mind told her she could not take anymore.

The pleasure was overwhelming. Her sensitive sex pulsated, and Journey desperately wanted to squeeze her legs together for some semblance of relief.

Archie nipped at her thighs. "You can take it. We're not done, *cariad*," he murmured, giving her sex one last kiss that had her crashing into wave of bliss.

Journey was barely aware of the kisses crawling up her body. The swirl of his tongue over one of her nipples had her moaning, offering herself to him.

He licked a path to her neck. Journey did not recognize the sounds coming from her own mouth. "Archie, please...more." She had no idea what she was begging for, but she wanted more.

"Dear God, you're glorious. I want to spend the rest of my life pleasing you." He kissed her rough and hard. The taste of her essence on his tongue drove her wild. She had never done anything so scandalous in her twenty years of life.

Journey tried to ignore the meaning of his words. He couldn't please her for the rest of his life because she was leaving him. She had to...didn't she?

Archie pressed his forehead against hers, his eyes searching, "Tell me you want this, *cariad*."

Cupping his cheek with her hand, she could feel the prickle of a beard. Her heart soared, eyes watering as she told him the truest words that she had ever said. "I want this. I want you, Archie."

Grabbing her by the nape, he pulled her to him, kissing her, claiming her. Taking his manhood he lined his member to her overheated sex, thrusting forward, firm but gentle. Journey no longer cared. She just wanted him, only him. Her arms wrapped around his wide shoulders tighter as her sex stretched to accommodate his impressive length. The slight burn caused water to pull in her already teary eyes, so she closed them, taking several deep breaths as he pushed in further.

"That's it. Take me in," he whispered against her lips, the erotic words coaxing her legs further apart.

She could feel herself become even wetter as he settled in between her legs, unable to go any further. He was fully seated inside of her, and it was magnificent.

His body shook as he stayed connected to her, but she needed him to move. She pulsed around his manhood, feeling more empowered than she ever had.

"J-Journey, I need a moment." His voice shook from his efforts to control himself, but she needed him desperately.

Pulling him by the hair, she licked his lips, looking into his eyes. "No. I need you now, Archie."

"Fuck." He released the curse before he crashed his lips into hers.

Journey only had a moment to prepare herself for the onslaught of his thrusts. He was relentless as he lifted one of her legs, moving in and out of her, their tongues never leaving each other. Her hands roamed down his taut back, taking in the sinewy muscles until she reached his firm backside, squeezing and kneading as he had done hers earlier.

Archie let out a sound that sounded very much like a growl to Journey as her sex gripped his shaft. Crying out, her head fell back as her sensitive body began to quiver and pulse... again. She could not count how many times he had caused her pleasure. Surely it was unheard of.

"Oh, Archie!" she called out as she crashed against the rocks of pleasure.

"Yes, that's it, *cariad*." Archie sat up, taking hold of her waist as he thrusted repeatedly.

Journey gripped the bedsheets as another wave of pleasure assaulted her. She shook her head, feeling as if she could not take another orgasm.

"Journey!" He cried out her name, his head thrown back in the throes of pleasure.

He was a spectacular sight to behold, and for the first time in her life, she cared for someone other than herself and her family.

Chapter Ten

Asennight after their night together, Archie found himself walking through Hyde Park, Journey beside him, Emma running ahead with Felix, the puppy they had discovered at the inn in Wales. It was a beautiful spring day, and though he could feel the stares of society on him, he found that he did not care.

Archie had not had a single care in the world since his night with Journey. She was everything that he had been missing in his life for the past nine years. He hadn't thought it was possible to find love again after Katherine, but he had.

It was different; the two women Archie had fallen in love with were like night and day. Katherine was wild and did not care for rules or anything really. It was Archie who had grounded them both. Journey was kind, filled with fire, passion, and so much love; she pushed Archie to be better. She was beautiful and everything he wanted in a wife, but he could still feel that she was keeping something from him.

They walked Rotten Row in Hyde Park. Though it was not the fashionable hour, they still gained the attention of a few members of society. Archie could not blame them, of course. He would've stared at Journey, too, if he had seen her before she became Emma's governess.

She was radiant in a blue pelisse and bonnet that hid her pretty face, yet you could still see the smooth brown skin and wild mane of hair peeping out.

Archie admired Journey as she watched Emma run ahead holding the small leash around Felix's neck. "My mother sent word and will join us this evening for dinner."

Journey's sun-kissed eyes found his, and dear God, he wanted to kiss her in front of all of London.

"Your mother? How wonderful." Hurt and hesitation flashed in her eyes before she looked away. "I shall have my dinner in my room."

Taking hold of her elbow, he turned her to face him. "No, you misunderstand. I would like you to meet my mother."

A tight smile formed on her kissable lips. "I have met The Dowager Lady Aberdeen before when she hired me as Emma's governess."

He took a step forward, aware that he was going against propriety. "Yes, I am aware, but this time I do not want you to meet her as Emma's governess. I want you to meet her as my fia—"

"Aberdeen! I thought that was you," Richmore's booming voice interrupted Archie's poor attempt at a proposal. "Why haven't you sent word that you arrived?" His friend slapped him on the back several times, which was their usual greeting.

The Duke of Richmore stood taller than Archie with a full crop of blonde hair. His wide girth was a shock to anyone who was not familiar with him. Gray eyes danced from Journey to Archie full of questions which Archie ignored.

Archie looked at one of his oldest and dearest friends, joy filling him. He hadn't seen Richmore in nearly two years when he had traveled to Wales for Emma's birthday. "Richmore, we only arrived a few days ago. I would've sent word, but we had been busy with Lady Emma's new puppy."

In truth the blasted thing wouldn't stop whining, keeping nearly the entire house awake, so much so that Archie had only been able to visit Journey one night out of the three they had been in London.

"We?" Richmore asked, tilting his head toward Journey, who was watching Emma most dutifully.

"Allow me to introduce Miss Beaumont, m-my—"

"Lady Emma's governess." Journey interrupted his stammering. "It is an honor to meet you, Your Grace."

Richmore, ever the duke, bowed to Journey, displaying a perfect set of white teeth. "The honor is mine to meet such an enchanting lady."

Archie watched color bloom on Journey's cheek, feeling a sting of jealousy towards his old friend. "Save your flattery for the ballroom. I'm sure the ladies are eager to catch your attention this season."

Richmore let out a rich hearty laugh. "They are, but you my friend are the catch of the season, especially with your mother advertising to anyone who will listen that you are in want of a new marchioness after all this time."

"Surely you jest?" Archie could feel Journey stiffen beside him before she excused herself and went to Emma who was playing happily with her new puppy.

"I do not. I believe she is throwing a ball in your honor in a sennight." Richmore looked over at Journey who was bending down to pet Felix. "But I dare say you have already been captured by a certain governess. Dear God, who could blame you? She is beautiful."

Archie followed his gaze watching as Journey interacted with Emma. "She is. She's also smart and kind and has a fierce temper."

"You're in love with her?" he asked, his voice full of wonder.

Facing his friend, Archie could not deny it any longer. He had been fascinated with Journey since the moment she stepped into Plas Castle, but he had fallen in love with her slowly through their constant bickering. With every touch, every kiss, she had claimed him mind, body, and soul. "Yes."

"Bloody hell, and here I thought that this season would be unbearable." He clapped his gloved hands together, smiling as if he'd won a game of whist. "The Marquess of Aberdeen marrying his governess...it'll be the scandal of the century. I wish it was me."

Archie shook his head at his friend, wishing he could punch him in his abnormally large jaw. "Be quiet," Archie commanded, as he tried to conceal his smile.

He had missed Richmore. He had always been like the brother he never had.

"In all seriousness, I'm happy for you my friend." Richmore placed his hand on Archie's shoulder, giving it a squeeze.

"She hasn't said yes yet." Archie reminded him, worry gripping at his heart.

What if she said no?

"I believe she will." Richmore bowed his head toward Archie. "Will I see you in Parliament?" He waited for Archie's answer.

Archie did not hesitate in his reply. He had a reason to fight now, and he would do anything for her. "Yes."

~

ARCHIE KNOCKED on Journey's door before dinner wanting to speak with her. She had disappeared to the safety of her room as soon as they had returned. This was Archie's opportunity for a moment alone with Journey, and perhaps this time he wouldn't ruin it completely.

Journey opened the door, holding the pink gown she wore their first night together. Moving aside she allowed him to come in, though he no longer cared what others thought of their engagement. She would soon be his wife, and there was no one in the world who could stop them from being together.

When he entered the room, he noticed her trunk and valise being filled with dresses and gowns. A sharp pain pierced his chest, the ache spreading throughout his body.

"What are you doing, Journey?" His voice sounded distant to his own ears.

Fear gripped him as he watched her meticulously fold the gown and place it inside of her trunk. She was silent as she walked over to the wardrobe filled with her clothes.

"Answer me, please," he begged as he walked over to her, stopping her from taking another dress out the wardrobe.

"You came to London to find a wife?" she asked, staring him in the eye. Fire burned in her gaze, and he wanted desperately to look away, but he couldn't. He needed her to know the truth.

"Yes, I did intend to marry this season." He took a step forward, taking her hand in his. "I thought it was time to give my daughter a mother, but I realized that I didn't need to travel all this way for a wife."

"Why?" Her voice quivered, so unlike the strong woman he'd known for a few short months.

Archie knelt on one knee, looking up at her. "Because my daughter already has a mother in you, Journey. Please do me the honor of becoming my marchioness."

He waited for her answer, watching her closely as the tears fell. No words were said as she released his hands and turned away from him.

"I can't marry you Archie." Her whispered reply broke his heart in two.

"Journey—" He started to protest, beg, do anything for her to be his wife, to be Emma's mother.

"I'm leaving England in less than four months. I'm going back to Jamaica once I receive my inheritance."

Wordlessly, Archie stumbled to the chaise, barely falling onto the seat. He was dizzy with rage and betrayal. He couldn't believe that Journey had deceived him in such a way. "What inheritance?" He searched her face. Seeing her drained of color did nothing to sooth his aching heart.

"I am to inherit my father's entire fortune. The plantation, the shipping company—everything was left to me, but I don't want it." She spit the words out, shaking her head.

He could see her body shaking with rage, as she spoke of her father's business. He knew how much she loathed the slave trade. There was no way that she would own another person.

"You knew this, yet you still accepted the position as Emma's governess?" Lies. She had lied to him about everything, and he'd believed her.

"I have to leave England. My father's business partner is determined to marry me. My father named him my guardian until I come of age at one and twenty." She swiped her tears angrily. "I've been running from him for two years. I won't marry Ramsay, and I'll die before I allow him to gain position of White Rose Plantation and all its enslaved men and women."

"Ramsay?" he asked, not believing that the world would be so small.

"Yes. Do you know him?"

He watched as she folded her arms across her chest. Archie couldn't believe that Ramsay was the cause of Journey's despair.

He would do everything in his power to prevent Journey

from marrying Bernard Ramsay. He knew Ramsay well, too well in his opinion.

"Yes, he's Katherine's older brother and Emma's uncle." He watched as she stumbled over her own two feet.

Running to her, Archie took her in his arms and led her to the chaise.

Chapter Eleven

The room was whirling wildly before Journey's eyes, and she could feel herself drifting toward the floor until strong arms wrapped around her. Her breathing was coming out in shallow pants. She couldn't get enough air into her lungs to breathe properly. Journey's skin was cold and clammy. She was going to be ill. There was no other explanation for how she was feeling.

Trying to compose herself and not swoon in front of Archie like an English debutante, Journey clutched at her chest, desperate for relief and air. Her world had been turned upside down with the information that Bernard Ramsay was Archie's late wife's brother. No wonder Katherine was not involved in the Slave Trade Act—her brother, like Journey's father, had a direct interest in the slave trade. Their entire shipping company was built on it. Once the act was passed, their income had greatly decreased, nearly bankrupting Ramsay.

"Are you well, *cariad*?" His voice soothed her as he pulled her onto his lap, kissing the side of her head.

"Yes." She leaned her head on his shoulder closing her eyes as he rubbed up and down her back.

"You will not marry Ramsay, even if you refuse me—"

Journey's head snapped to his, her eyes blinking several times. He had proposed marriage to her, and all she could do was worry over Bernard Ramsay. A slither of hope filled her. She would be happy as Archie's wife and Emma's mother, but how could she have happiness when her family was enslaved?

"I would never refuse you, Archie. I-I can't turn my back on them and go live happily with you...no matter how much I would like to."

Archie gripped the nape of her hair, guiding her head back so that he was looking down at her. She was rendered speechless by the love and devotion in his heated gaze. "*Fy nghariad aur*, I would never ask you to abandon them. I'm asking you to be my wife, my partner, so that we are stronger together. We'll go to Jamaica and free every slave on your father's plantation. Once you secure their freedom and safety, we will return to England and continue the fight."

Journey closed her eyes allowing relief to wash over her. She couldn't love a person more than she loved Archie. "You would do that for me? Go to Jamaica and help me free them?"

Pushing back her wild mane of curls, he gave her one searing kiss, a promise of more to come. "Yes. I love you, and I never want to part from you."

Jumping in his arms, she covered his face in kisses. "I love you so much, Archie." Pressing her lips to his, Journey pressed herself closer to him, craving his warmth and strength.

Deepening the kiss, she forgot about her earlier sickness. Nothing else mattered, especially not Bernard Ramsay. They would face whatever obstacles may come their way together.

Lifting her into his strong arms, Archie walked over to the bed. Placing Journey on her feet, he cupped her face with both of his hands, slanting his mouth over hers repeatedly until she couldn't recall anything but him.

"Is that a yes, Miss Beaumont?" His heated gaze seared her

from the inside, a wicked gleam in his eyes. "Will you be my marchioness?"

"Yes, my lord," she whispered seductively against his lips, removing his tailcoat, letting it drop to the carpet.

His waistcoat was next as he deftly untied her day dress, their lips never parting. They were desperate in their pursuits to rid each other of their clothing.

Archie's hands on Journey's bare skin was a balm to her soul as they roamed and kneaded. Journey leaned back in his arms allowing him to devour her neck and breasts, her hand buried deep in his dark hair, pulling to the point of pain. He ignored the pain, teasing a nipple with his teeth. Journey cried out, pulling on his hair harder as he suckled her sensitive breast, his free hand cupping and massaging the other.

Journey traced a path down his firm chest to the peaks of his abdomen, down to his rigid manhood; it was thick and hard. As her fingers stroked over the silk-like skin, she tried to wrap her hand around his girth.

"If you keep doing that, I won't be able to have you, and I desperately need to be inside of you, now, *cariad*."

Sweet lord.

Journey's body clenched at his words, and she feared that she would orgasm where she stood. Instinctively his hand found her core, parting and diving into her wet heat.

"You're always so wet for me, so responsive." Teasing her swollen nub with his fingers, Journey's body shook nearly causing her to lose her balance again, but Archie's firm hold on her middle kept her cemented to him.

Removing his hand from her sex, he wet her bottom lip with her essence. She felt wanton and naughty as her tongue peeked out of her mouth, tasting his fingertips. He dipped the long appendage into her waiting mouth, groaning in pleasure as he watched her.

Wrenching his finger away, Archie crashed his mouth to

hers, lifting her in one fluid motion before he laid her onto the bed, sliding into her needy, wet heat.

Journey arched her back, crying out at the fullness of him as he began pounding her sex. She gripped his forearms, holding on to him as her thighs tightened around his waist. Her wanton cries of pleasure filled the room, and she wished she could contain them, but there was no use.

Archie pressed his much larger body to hers, kissing her wildly as his hold tightened around her middle. Flipping her over, he held on to her, guiding her hips in the new position.

"Ride me," he commanded, and she obeyed, following the movement of his hands as if he was leading her in a dance. "That's it, *cariad*." He released his hold on her hips, releasing her.

Swirling her hips, she found her own rhythm, chasing it, trying to capture the immense pleasure that was teasing her insides. Journey pushed herself up, sinking deeper onto his impressive length. His head tilted back in as he hissed through his teeth. His hands roamed her body, cupping her full breasts. He pinched and pulled at her sensitive nipples.

Pressing her hands into his chest, Journey bounced up and down on his long, hard shaft. The precipice of her completion was right in her reach, and dear God, did she want it. Only with him, her husband-to-be. Her body moved to its own music, Archie's hands cupping her bottom and guiding her.

Sitting up, he pressed his lips to hers in a fierce kiss, their movements becoming rough and chaotic. He pulled her harshly to him, going deeper into her core. She cried out, her hands going to his wide shoulder.

"Yes, yes." Once more Journey could not recognize her own voice. She had no idea what it was about Archie that made her forget herself. Her voice sounded strange to her own ears, but she had no time to consider the difference as Archie licked her nipple, sending sparks through her body directly to her core.

Journey had no warning as her body was hit with a ripple of completion that started in her core and climbed up her body until she was limp in his arms.

Archie's forceful movements didn't stop as he guided her on and off him. Journey pulled at his silky hair, needing to feel his lips on hers. She took his mouth, riding out another wave of pleasure, so full of love and devotion for the man in her arms.

He tightened his grip around her, slamming her down onto his member. Her name on his lips was the sweetest sound she had ever heard, and she would hear it for the rest of her life as his wife.

"I love you," she whispered in his ear as he kissed her bare shoulder.

"I love you, wife, now and forever." He smoothed her hair out of her face, pressing his lips to hers, and she felt complete.

They kissed, forgetting the outside world and its problems, only focusing on each other. A knock on the door shocked Journey. She looked toward it, hoping that the rest of the house did not hear them.

"M-my Lord, you have a visitor," a maid called out to Archie.

"Thank you, Louisa," Archie said in a stern voice, not hinting that he was still buried inside of Journey.

She hid her head in his neck, trying to hide herself from the embarrassment that the entire house knew he was in there with her in the middle of the day. She just hoped Emma was nowhere to be found.

Archie stroked up her back, gripping her neck so that he could look into her eyes. "No more secrets, wife." He rubbed his nose against hers.

She smiled feeling happier than she ever had before. "No more secrets."

~

ARCHIE WALKED through his home with a permanent smile on his face. He was going to be married as soon as humanly possible. He couldn't wait to make Journey his wife, to start a new life with her. For years he had only survived for Emma, a shadow of his former self. Now he was alive, happy, and in love.

He entered the drawing room with a wide smile on his face until he noticed the man that was waiting for him.

Bernard Ramsay.

He was a man twenty years' Archie's senior, his large build resembling a much younger man. Cool, calculating eyes surveyed Archie, taking in his slightly wrinkled clothing.

When Louisa informed him that he had a visitor, Archie rushed to dress, leaving the warm confines of Journey's thighs and the sweet taste of her kisses. Keeping his composure, he forced himself to face the man in front of him, wanting to rid their lives of him once and for all.

"Ramsay, what are you doing here?" Archie asked, not believing the man that Journey feared most was in his drawing room.

"Can an uncle not visit his niece?" he asked, a smug look on his face.

Archie never cared for Katherine's older brother. He was smug and devious and only cared for his own interests. It was no coincidence that he was standing in front of Archie like he was the Prince Regent.

"Not when you've never cared to pay her a visit in the nine years she has been alive." Archie took a seat, crossing his leg. "Tell me, why are you really here?" He wanted to make it clear to Ramsay that Journey was his, but he would take his time with that particular revelation.

Ramsay chuckled, shrugging his shoulder. "Very well. I saw you earlier with a woman of African descent that greatly favored my intended."

Archie feigned ignorance. "Your intended? I did not know you were to be married."

"Yes, my partner Beaumont's dying wish was that I see to his only child, and with no wife of my own, I see no reason why I cannot marry the girl." Ramsay sat down in a chair as if he had a claim to Journey.

"Perhaps because she doesn't want to marry you." Archie shrugged, watching as the other man stiffened.

He took great pleasure in Ramsay's discomfort. Ever since Journey had informed Archie that Ramsay was the reason why she had to leave her home and become a governess, he'd wanted to pummel the bastard.

"She is here." Ramsay stood, taking a step in Archie's direction. "Bring her to me now or—"

Having heard enough, Archie stood, towering over Ramsay. "Or what?" He challenged him. "What you're going do, Ramsay, is leave my house and never try to contact my daughter or my fiancé again."

Ramsay reeled back, his eyes closing into small slits as he glared at Archie. "You've had her—that is no concern of mine. I will have her, sullied and all."

"I'm not your property to have, Mr. Ramsay." Journey stood at the door, her hands clenched into fists by her side. She was a glorious sight. With her head held high and back straight, she strode across the room to stand in front of Ramsay who had turned to face her.

Archie had not heard her enter the drawing room as he was so focused on Ramsay. Not wanting Journey anywhere near the detestable man, Archie tried to stand in front of her, but she would not have it.

"Your father wished for you to be taken care of. I'm sure you're infatuated with Aberdeen, but you'll get over it." Ramsay gave her a sinister smile.

"My father was mistaken if he thought I would ever marry a man who would own another human being. Whatever you think you will gain by marrying me, you are mistaken." Journey folded her arms, the picture of strength and power.

Ramsay let out a humorless snort. "I'm sure Aberdeen has promised you many things, but I assure you he will not marry you. No matter what he has said, he's still in love with my dead sister."

Archie stepped forward, poking Ramsay in the chest with two fingers. "It's true I loved your sister very much, but I am in love with Miss Beaumont." Archie leaned into Ramsay, so only he could hear his next words. "Leave now or the information your father revealed to me will surface, and this time Katherine is not here to stop me."

Ramsay stumbled back, color draining from his face. "You wouldn't! The scandal would not only ruin me. Your family will be ruined by association."

"Perhaps, but it's a chance I'm willing to take for the woman I love." Archie stepped toward him. "Now get out of our home."

Ramsay looked from Archie to Journey before he stormed out of the drawing room, slamming the door behind him.

Archie faced Journey, taking in her wide eyes and open-mouthed expression. Closing the space between them, he took her in his arms and kissed her forehead. "He will never bother us again."

She pressed her hand against his chest, backing away from him slightly. "What just happened?" She raised her eyebrows, urging him to speak.

"I reminded him of some pertinent information I found years ago." Leading her over to the sofa, he sat her down before he continued. "Katherine's father and I became very close, and on his death bed, he told me the truth about his second son, Mr. Bernard Ramsay."

"W-what truth?" Her voice was breathless and anxious.

"Ramsay is not his father's son. His mother had an affair with a groomsman." Journey let out a loud gasp. "His father was out of the country for months, and when he returned, his wife was increasing. He knew the truth, but he never disowned Ramsay. His elder brother, however, does not hold Bernard Ramsay in high esteem and would disown him immediately."

Tears began streaming down Journey's face, her lip trembling. "I don't have to run anymore to keep my fortune?" she asked in a shocked voice.

"No, you don't have to run anymore. Your fortune is entirely yours to do what you've always wanted to do, *fy nghariad aur*." Archie wiped her tears away, basking in the fact that soon she would be his wife.

"We will free every slave at White Rose Plantation with my father's fortune." She gripped his forearms, a brilliant smile taking over her face.

"Yes, and when we're done in Jamaica, I will return to Parliament and work on freeing every slave in the Empire."

Journey pulled him to her, wrapping her arms around him, "Oh, Archie, do you really think we could do it?"

He kissed her neck, her cheek, and then her lips briefly, savoring. "I do. I think we can do anything as long we do it together."

Her smile lit up the world as her sun-kissed brown eyes stared up at him. "Together."

Epilogue

Wales, September 1833

Archie leapt out of the still moving carriage as it pulled in front of Plas Castle. He had been in London the entire season working on the Slavery Abolition Act. This Act would abolish slavery in most British colonies. It is what Archie had wanted from the moment he began fighting with the abolitionist movement.

Journey had insisted that he attend Parliament even with her carrying their fifth child. He had not wanted to leave her so near her confinement, the fear from losing Kathcrine still lingering in the back of his mind. He couldn't lose Journey. She was his entire world, the reason he woke up in the morning with a permanent smile on his face.

They had been married a fortnight after his confrontation with Ramsay. His mother insisted on having the proper time to plan the wedding breakfast of the season. Journey's grandmother had arrived from Kent along with her uncle, Viscount Wiltmore, who had never taken an interest in Journey before.

After Journey turned twenty-one, they traveled to Jamaica

where she was reunited with her mother's siblings. Archie remembered the scene as if it were yesterday. Her cousins had seen them first, running and taking Journey in her arms. Tears had assaulted Archie as her aunt and uncles surrounded her, all wrought with emotion.

Running into the castle past Henrietta, who had assumed the post of head housekeeper more than eight years earlier, Archie did not stop, allowing his legs to move as though he were a younger man and not a man eight and forty.

"Papa! You've returned," Ini, he and Journey's eldest daughter who was named after Journey's mother, ran into his arms. He lifted her slightly off the ground, swinging her around. She was tall for her ten years, dark thick hair like Archie's, laid in curls down her back.

"We've missed you so, Papa," Emma said, kissing his cheek. She was now the Duchess of Claybourn, but he still saw his little girl whenever he looked at her. She was the spitting image of her mother, but her mannerisms and heart were that of Journey.

"I've missed you all too, *fy mach i*. Where is your mother?" he asked, trying not to rush past his girls whom he missed dearly. Especially Emma who he rarely saw since she was now a married duchess.

"They're upstairs! Wait until you see—" Ini started but was cut off by Emma.

"She's upstairs resting." Emma spoke over Ini. "Come, Ini. Claybourn is waiting for us at the stables." Before she walked away, Emma turned to him. "Did it pass, father?" she asked hurriedly, knowing the importance of what Archie had spent years fighting for.

"I will inform everyone after I speak to your mother." Archie left his daughters hurriedly, rushing through the castle to get to his wife. The castle was now filled with former enslaved men and women who had chosen to return with them and work for their wages. Others went their own way. Both of Journey's uncles had stayed at White Rose, turning it into a working plantation where the workers received actual wages.

Reaching the family wing, Archie's heart beat rapidly out of his chest as he ignored the fear that crept up his spine.

"You've returned!" yelled Claire who was named after Archie's own mother. At seven years, she was the spitting image of her mother with smooth brown skin, light-brown eyes, and dark-brown curls.

"Papa!" Jane, their youngest at five years, wrapped herself around Archie's leg.

Lifting her up, he kissed her cheek, taking in the dark hair and blue eyes that most resembled him.

"Girls, how I've missed you, but I must go find your mama." Sitting Jane down he rose as Irie, Journey's cousin and the girls' nursemaid, walked up, looking sternly at the girls.

"Come, you two. No more escaping the nursery or no biscuits." She was a tall, lean commanding figure who demanded the children's respect. "Well, did it pass?" Her intense brown eyes pierced him, but he stood firm in his decision not to say anything until after he spoke to his wife.

Archie shook his head, standing. "First my wife." It was difficult keeping such news that affected practically everyone.

"Then go to her and your newborn child." Irie ushered the girls away, leaving Archie speechless.

Child?

Without thinking Archie ran to the duchess's rooms, shoving the doors open. Stumbling in, he righted himself, meeting the tired gaze of his beautiful wife.

Journey sat on the bed holding a small bundle in her arms. He couldn't form a single word or comprehend anything other than her and the babe in her arms. They were alive and well.

Her last letter mentioned nothing of her confinement or her labor. She had kept one last secret from him. She knew how important passing the Slavery Abolition Act was for their family and enslaved people all over the Empire.

"Good, you're here. Did it pass?" Aunt Femi placed her hand on her wide hips. She was a skilled midwife who had assisted Journey with the birth of every one of their children.

"Auntie, let him breathe. He's only just arrived." Journey's voice was firm but kind.

Femi let out a smacking sound with her lips, walking out of the room with the speed of a much younger person.

Sitting beside his wife. Archie bent to kiss her, savoring and tasting before he took the babe out of her arms, looking down at the cherubic face. Tears filled his eyes. Even after four children, holding one of them for the first time would always be one of the happiest moments of his life.

Archie couldn't recall the many names they had written back and forth about for months. All he saw was a shock of jet-black hair and a tiny nose.

"Well?" His wife pressed, wanting to know the outcome of the Act.

Looking up at her, he raised a brow. "Do I not get a moment to enjoy my daughter?"

She chuckled, and dear Lord, did he miss the sound of her laughter. "Your son."

He blinked several times, trying to comprehend her words. He had long given up on having an heir. He was happy with his daughters and was hoping for a grandson to pass his title to as there were no males in his line. "My son?"

"Yes." The reply was simple, taking Archie out of his stupor.

"Perhaps we should try for a spare or another daughter." He teased her after he kissed his son on the forehead.

"Archibald Huxley, did it pass?" She gritted out the words, becoming vexed with him.

He looked over at her, taking in her stern face. She was so beautiful, and he never got tired of staring at her, his strong, determined wife. "We did it," he whispered the words as she took his hand in hers.

Archie watched as a flood of emotion traveled over her—relief, joy, and victory the most prominent one of all. The tears that fell were well fought and won. He could have never done anything without her by his side, pushing him to be better and do better.

A smile took over her face as she squeezed his hand. "We did it."

The End.

Acknowledgments

First, I would like to thank God for everything he does and continues to do for me. Without him I'm confident that this book would not have been finished. Not only did I finish writing, but I also was able to have it beta read, edited, formatted, proofread and uploaded on time. Yessss!

Thank you to the Regency in Color ladies for allowing me to jump in on this ride! I've had my eye on RIC for a year and I went after it, as I tend to do for all things. Thank you all so much for allowing me to tell Journey & Archie's story!

To my family, my husband and son, thanks for dealing with me, and being so understanding when I start screaming, 'I have to finish this book!' Thank you both for being understanding (a tiny bit!) Thanks to my brother, niece, nephews & Maya for allowing me time to write in between visits. Thanks to my mother, who only called twice a day when I was sprinting. Finally, thanks to my loyal companion, Sadie, the best dog in the world for taking walks whenever I wasn't sprinting.

To my friends,
Thank you all for your unwavering love and support. Without you all I would surely quit everything, every day. To all my sprinting ladies, and my sprinting Facebook group, thank you so much for sprinting with me, it really has helped me stay on track and get all the words. To my daily sprinting partner,

Addy, I would surely not make a word count or have a good story without you.

To Debbie & V you two are really the best cheerleaders anyone could ask for. Thanks for always believing in me, even when I don't believe in myself.

To Cheryl & Pamela, thank you so much for always supporting me and dealing with my daily drama. None of my work would be readable without you two.

To April, thanks for being my emergency grammar check, and reader. You're a constant and the most solid person I know.

This book would not be complete without the help of every single person mention and some not mentioned. It takes a village to publish a book! Lastly, thanks to my VA Lexi, who always helps me with valuable advice. Thanks to all the authors I've met on this journey. You all rec me and allow me into your groups. You all are so wonderful and kind and I'm glad to be a part of this wonderful world!

More by Cecilia Rene

The Bachelor Duke
https://www.amazon.com/Bachelor-Duke-Book-ebook/dp/B08DMPWK9V

Ruined by The Bachelor Marquess
https://www.amazon.com/gp/product/B08T6VX93D

Forever Her Bachelor
Releasing 2023

Regency in Color Series

Read the entire series here
https://www.amazon.com/dp/B09QKJ6X66

An Excerpt from Merry Farmer

Regency in Color Book 11
THE FORTY-DAY GOVERNESS

BY

Mary Farmer

Copyright ©2022 by Merry Farmer

This book is a work of fiction. Names, characters, places, and incidents are products of the author's imagination or are used fictitiously. Any resemblance to actual events or locales or persons, living or dead, is entirely coincidental.

Cover design by Erin Dameron-Hill (who is completely fabulous)

ASIN: B0B5HFNK72
Paperback: 9798842747771

Click here for a complete list of other works by Merry Farmer.

If you'd like to be the first to learn about when the next books in the series come out and more, please sign up for my newsletter here: http://eepurl.com/RQ-KX

$$\mathcal{The\ Forty-Day}$$
$$\mathcal{Governess}$$

CHAPTER ONE

Kingston, Jamaica – May, 1820

It wasn't the worst possible situation Matthew Weatherly, newly minted Earl of Westbrook, could have found himself in, but it was close.

"...and once again, Lord Westbrook, I am sorry for your loss," Mr. Earnshaw said with an obsequious smile as he shook Matthew's hand, sealing the sale of his deceased brother's plantation.

"Thank you so much, Mr. Earnshaw," Matthew replied with a bow and an uncertain smile. "May you find as much happiness and prosperity with my brother's land as he did."

"Oh, I am quite certain I will, my lord." Earnshaw bowed to him, then turned and marched out of the drawing room where they had finalized the terms of the sale, chuckling to himself as he did.

Matthew watched the man leave with a sense of uncertainty. Had he truly done the right thing in selling his brother's plantation? He'd bent over backwards to make certain Earnshaw shared his views on abolition and that he would treat the men and women who had worked for his brother with fairness and equanimity, but one could never be certain about such things in the current environment.

And that was without the worry that he was robbing his orphaned nieces, Hibiscus and Heliconia—George's wife had insisted on naming their twin daughters after native flowers of Jamaica as she lay dying after their birth—of their birthright.

"That was a tidy business," George's friend, the Marquess of Quintrell, said, approaching Matthew with a smile. Matthew supposed Quintrell was his friend now as well, seeing as he had so kindly offered his home not only as a place to conduct the business of the sale, but where he and the twins could reside after vacating George's house for the sale months before. "You fetched a remarkable price for the place."

Matthew hummed doubtfully and turned to face Quintrell fully. "But was it enough to provide for Hibby and Helly?" he asked, his brow furrowed and his shoulders tight. "By all rights, it should have been their land and their home."

"Nonsense," Quintrell laughed, gesturing for Matthew to follow him out onto the porch, where one of the dark-skinned house servants was waiting with glasses of refreshing punch for them. "Girls cannot inherit. Your brother's property—here and in England—is yours by right of birth. You are an extraordinary man for considering those girls above your own aims."

Matthew opened his mouth to express that the twins would always be his first concern, and that he had never imagined in his wildest dreams that he would end up with the title and land that had been in his family's possession for centuries.

Quintrell bowled right over him with, "I am quite certain that those girls are in the very best of hands, after their father's sudden demise, and that they will grow up to be fine young women with large dowries that will make their future husbands quite happy."

Quintrell laughed and slapped Matthew's back just as he began to take a drink of punch. The result was that he spilled a great deal of it down his front.

"Blast," Matthew muttered, searching around for something to dab it away with.

"Kyria," Quintrell called out to a woman who happened to be passing from one of the outbuildings into the main house at the far end of the porch. "Would you be so kind as to fetch something for Lord Westbrook to clean himself up with?"

Matthew's heart fluttered against his ribs as Quintrell brought attention to him. Or perhaps the nervous sensation was because of the no-nonsense look Miss Kingston sent him before saying, "Yes, sir," nodding, then stepping into the house.

There was something about Miss Kyria Kingston that had made Matthew nervous from the moment they'd first met months ago, when he'd arrived on the island. She seemed to be a solid fixture in Quintrell's house, though not as any ordinary sort of servant. She was always impeccably dressed in the very latest fashions and groomed to a degree that would make the ladies of the ton green with jealousy. Miss Kingston was orderliness and organization personified, and even Quintrell's housekeeper seemed to bow to her opinions on the running of the house and everything surrounding it.

Of course, it did not require much of an imagination to determine who Miss Kingston truly was and why she received such favor in Quintrell's house. The resemblance she bore to Quintrell, despite her darker complexion, was striking. Matthew might not have been as world-wise or sophisticated as George and many of his peers were, but he knew enough about the things that were unspoken to guess at Miss Kingston's origins.

"I fear I know nothing at all about being a member of the peerage," Matthew sighed his thoughts aloud as he watched the doorway Miss Kingston had disappeared through.

A moment later, he jerked straight, face heating at his untimely admission.

"I...er...that is, I had no expectations of ever finding myself in the position I am in now," he blundered on, sending Quintrell an apologetic look. "I am the third son, you see," he explained. "George was the oldest, and I always believed that if anything were to happen to him, our brother Henry would have inherited everything."

"Yes, I was sorry to hear of Henry's death as well," Quintrell said. "I knew him through George. He always seemed like a jolly fellow."

"Too jolly, as it turned out," Matthew sighed, feeling a wave of grief. "He never should have attempted to jump that hedge."

And Matthew should never have been saddled with a mountain of responsibilities he was neither educated nor prepared for. He'd always expected to become a scholar or inventor of some sort. Perhaps even a physician. Before George and Henry had died, back when there were no expectations on his shoulders at all, he had filled his days with investigations into all of the latest medical advances that were being made in England and throughout Europe. He'd imagined himself becoming some sort of apprentice to a surgeon in London, or even practicing medicine himself. He'd wished he'd learned more about tropical diseases when word reached him that George had succumbed to a tropical fever all those months ago.

All of that was in the past now. He'd become the Earl of

Westbrook, and the expectations on his shoulder were now of a different sort entirely.

"You are fortunate to have concluded the business of the land sale before your ship departs tomorrow," Quintrell said, gesturing for the attending servant to hand Matthew another glass of punch. "That was cutting it a bit close, wasn't it?"

"It was," Matthew said with a wary look. In fact, he'd been terrified that he wouldn't be able to complete George's business before the *Anthem* set sail for England, and that he would either have to stay another few months in Jamaica—something he was loath to do, knowing how much business awaited him at home in Exeter—or leaving before everything had been settled. He thanked the heavens that he didn't have anything to worry about now.

As if the gods and angels had heard his thoughts and felt it necessary to joke with him, a flurry of noise and movement at the end of the patio caught his attention, and his nieces came tearing toward him.

"Uncle Matthew, Uncle Matthew, is it true we are in danger of being captured by pirates?" Helly asked, her blue eyes wide with horror, as she and Hibby stumbled to a stop on either side of him. They grabbed his hands as if for dear life.

Despite everything, Matthew laughed and his insides filled with light and hope. "Who told you that?" he asked, beaming at the two girls.

"Johnny Marshall told us," Hibby said, her eyes just as wide as Helly's.

"Johnny Marshall?" Matthew glanced to Quintrell in question.

Quintrell laughed. "He's the son of George's plantation manager."

"Oh, I see." Matthew smiled and crouched so that he could be at eye level with the twins. "We shall not be captured by pirates," he told them, trying to sound stern and authoritative, which he was not generally good at. "And if they dare to come near us, I will take up arms...and make certain that you both take them up as well, as you are both far fiercer than I am."

The girls laughed and squealed with delight. So much so that Quintrell winced.

"I think I should carry a sword on the ship," Helly said. "That way the pirates will know to stay away."

"Could I have one too?" Hibby asked. "I should very much like to stab things."

Matthew laughed out loud. His nieces were a bit wild, it was true, but he adored their spirit and rather thought that the three of them would be happy together. They were only just seven years old, but the two of them had been through so much in their young lives, and they were remarkably intelligent for their age. Perhaps that was because George had always valued learning and had hired a governess for them at the earliest possible age.

That governess, Miss Benning, stumbled onto the end of the patio at that moment, as if she had been chasing after the girls and had only just caught up to them.

"No swords for the two of you, I think," Matthew said, rising and resting a hand on each of their heads. They both groaned and complained about that, until Matthew said, "Not until I teach you how to properly fight with a sword."

The twins gasped and lit up at the prospect.

"You would teach us?" Hibby asked.

"Truly?" Helly followed.

"We shall see," Matthew said, smiling amiably as Miss Benning walked stiffly toward them. "Miss Benning might want to teach you herself."

"Miss Benning will do no such thing, my lord," the governess said, a sharp edge in her voice as she reached their group.

"Oh, dear," Matthew said, sensing the woman's unhappiness and guessing what might happen.

Miss Benning took in a breath and faced him squarely. "My lord, I have thought long and hard about this, and I regret that I have not given you sufficient notice, but I refuse to go to England with you and these—" She snapped her mouth shut rather than continuing, which Matthew thought was likely for the best, judging by the contempt the woman clearly had for his nieces. She took another breath, then said, "I have tried in vain to teach these two hellions manners and decorum, but they are two of the naughtiest, most unmanageable little girls I have ever known."

"Hold on there," Matthew said, handing his new glass of punch back to the servant who had delivered it and pulling his nieces in closer to his sides. "They are young, is all, and they have just been orphaned."

"Yes," Helly said, putting on a decidedly pathetic expression as she hugged Matthew's side. "We have just been orphaned."

Hibby burst into false tears, which Matthew thought was laying it on a bit thick. He understood what Miss Benning meant by calling the girls unruly.

"I am very sorry for their loss, Lord Westbrook, but I cannot continue on as their governess," Miss Benning said. "Particularly as it would mean being confined to close quarters with them for the voyage, which I hear can take up to forty days."

The woman looked as though she would go on and express all her misgivings in a torrent of emotion, but Matthew stopped her.

"I thank you for your service, Miss Benning, and I accept your resignation," he said. "I would just ask that you remain in our service for one day more, until we board the *Anthem*.

And, if you would, could you take the girls off to have their tea now while I conclude business here?"

Miss Benning sighed, though Matthew couldn't tell if it was with exasperation or relief. "Yes, my lord," she said, then held her hands out for the twins. "Come along girls."

Once again, the twins whined in protest.

"Do we have to go?" Hibby asked, batting her eyelashes up at him.

Matthew laughed at her manipulations. "Yes, my dears, you do," he said. He leaned over and kissed each of their foreheads. "Go have your tea, then prepare to embark on the journey of your life tomorrow."

That seemed to appease the girls. They squealed and jumped up and down, hugging Matthew tightly.

"Uncle Matthew, you've spilled punch on your nice jacket," Helly said as she stepped away to go with Miss Benning. "You know you mustn't spill things on yourself."

Matthew laughed. "Thank you for informing me, my dear. But see? Miss Kingston is here with a towel so that I can clean up."

The twins seemed satisfied with that and allowed themselves to be led away by Miss Benning.

Miss Kingston stepped forward to offer the small towel. Matthew wasn't certain how long she'd been back on the porch or how much of his interaction with his nieces she'd witnessed, but now that he knew she was there, the fluttery feeling in his gut returned.

"Thank you, Miss Kingston," he said, taking the towel from her with a smile. "You are as efficient as you are—" He stopped. It would have been outrageously improper for him to say she was beautiful, even though she was. Miss Kingston was not the sort of woman to blush and stammer at compliments, though. She was far too serious and commanding for that.

"Thank you for saying so, Lord Westbrook," she said, taking a step back. She met Matthew's eyes without reservation, as if she wasn't intimidated by his title or his nationality, or anything else about him. She was respectful, and Matthew had the impression that she liked him well enough, which was more than she owed to him, if he were being honest with himself.

"You've taken on quite a load with those girls," Quintrell laughed as Matthew did a more thorough job of tidying his jacket.

"They're perfectly lovely, though," he said, smiling.

"They are, but they need a mother." Quintrell nodded. "And you need a countess."

Matthew sighed. "I'm afraid I do." He finished with the towel and handed it back to Miss Kingston with a grateful smile, then turned to Quintrell. "I always assumed I'd marry one day, when I found a woman I fancied. I never had ambitions of marrying for position or to form an alliance of great families. I've always just wanted to be happy in my domestic life."

Quintrell laughed. "I know that feeling, my lord. It is possible for a second marriage, as I have recently come to consider myself."

Miss Kingston stared suddenly at Quintrell, her eyes going wide.

"But not for a man in the position you are in," Quintrell continued. "Mark my words, Westbrook, you need to find yourself a wife of good breeding as quickly as possible. Those girls need supervision and a mother's touch, and you need guidance from a woman well-versed in the *ton* and everything it implies."

"I do," Matthew sighed. "I know absolutely nothing about the position I find myself in. I need tutelage in all things having to do with society and the aristocracy."

"Lady Irene Sudbury," Quintrell said, as though announcing the woman's arrival at a ball.

"I beg your pardon?" Matthew said, shaking his head and blinking rapidly.

"Lady Irene Sudbury," Quintrell repeated. "I've taken the liberty of perusing the passenger list for the *Anthem*. Lady Irene Sudbury is the widow of the late Earl of Sudbury. Her husband succumbed to the same fever that took George, and she is now returning to her family in England. She is the perfect countess for you as she is already the Countess of Sudbury."

"Oh, I suppose she is," Matthew said.

"She would be able to instruct you in everything you need to know as an earl, and as she is childless herself—she was only married to Sudbury for a year before his demise, you see, and he was nearly twice as old as her—she would be an ideal mother to George's little hellions."

"Yes, I suppose so," Matthew said, rubbing his chin as he considered it. "I have not been introduced to her yet."

Quintrell shrugged. "A minor inconvenience. You will be introduced tomorrow, I am certain, once you are settled on the *Anthem*."

"I suppose you're right." Matthew shifted his stance as another thought struck him. "What I need more immediately than a wife is a governess for the twins," he said. "It is damnably inconvenient that I need to find one on such short notice. I doubt whether I will be able to find a qualified candidate willing to leave everything to set out for England in less than twenty-four hours at all."

"Nonsense," Quintrell said, his smile growing wider. "Miss Kingston will go with you as governess for the girls."

"What is this?" Matthew said, stunned.

"I beg your pardon?" Miss Kingston said at the exact same time.

The two of them exchanged a look as though neither could truly believe what Quintrell had suggested.

Quintrell spread his hands as though he'd made the winning argument in a court case. "You need a competent and reliable governess for the voyage to England," he explained. "Miss Kingston is available, and a daresay she would enjoy exploring life in England, especially with the introductions and support both you and I could give her."

"I have no desire to explore England," Miss Kingston said, speaking to Quintrell in a manner that Matthew found extraordinarily familiar...and further proof of what the connection between the two of them truly was. "I have ambitions here," she said, eyeing Quintrell with particular intensity.

"Now, now, my dear," Quintrell said to her. "Not all of our ambitions can be fulfilled the way we might want them to be. Lord Westbrook is in great need. You would be doing him a service."

Miss Kingston pressed her lips together, let out a breath through her nose, then turned to Matthew with a far softer, kinder look. "It is not that I have no wish to help Lord Westbrook in his time of need—"

"Good," Quintrell said. "That's settled then. I shall have Marian pack your trunk immediately."

"But—"

"The voyage is only forty days, my dear," Quintrell cut her off again. "If you do not like England once you get there, it will be but another forty days for you to return. I will provide you with letters of introduction to my kin in England, not to mention a sizable purse that will help you see to your every need for as long as you are on those foreign shores."

Miss Kingston still didn't look certain. She peeked at Matthew for a moment, then frowned at Quintrell. "May I speak to you in private?" she asked, her jaw clenched.

Quintrell sighed. "I suppose so." He gestured for Miss

Kingston to follow him into the house. "I will sort this matter for you, Lord Westbrook, never fear. Proceed with your plans for departure."

"I...I will, sir," Matthew told the man with a nod.

He watched as Quintrell and Miss Kingston disappeared into the house, and heard Miss Kingston's low, irritated voice as she spoke, without hearing the words. He hated to engage a governess for the twins who was unwilling, but in the last few months he had observed that the girls liked Miss Kingston. And there was every indication that Miss Kingston would make a fine governess. She was intelligent and brooked no nonsense, which, Matthew had to admit, the girls needed.

Yes, he decided, Miss Kingston would make the perfect governess for the voyage home. And once they reached English shores, he would do whatever he could to ensure she was happy. Perhaps, while he was at it, Miss Kingston might assist him in winning the attention of Lady Sudbury as well, for if there was one thing Matthew knew for certain, it was that he didn't have the slightest idea how to woo a countess.

Secrets with the
Marquess Bibliography

Slavery and the British transatlantic slave trade
The National Archives
https://www.nationalarchives.gov.uk/help-with-your-research/research-guides/british-transatlantic-slave-trade-records/

Slavery Abolition Act
  Britannica
  https://www.britannica.com/topic/Slavery-Abolition-Act

The English Conquest of Jamaica
  By Carla Gardina Pestana
  The Belknap Press of Harvard university Press
  Cambridge, Massachusetts
  London, England 2017

Britain's Black Past
  By Gretchen H. Gerzina
  Liverpool University Press
  4 Cambridge Street

Liverpool L69 7ZU

Jamaica Ladies, Female Slaveholders and the Creation of Britain's Atlantic Empire
By Christine Walker
Omohundro Institute Of Early American History And Culture,
Williamsburg, Virginia, and the University of North Carolina Press,
Chapel Hill

Welsh Terms of Endearment
Omniglot
https://omniglot.com/language/endearment/welsh.htm

About Cecilia Rene

Cecilia Rene is a creative, happy, and outgoing Detroit native who majored in Broadcast Communication at Grambling State University. Immediately following her graduation, she started her new life in New York City. As a self-proclaimed New Yorker, her stimulating and diverse career in advertising sparked a drive for hard work and dedication. Her love and passion for writing followed her from childhood through adulthood, where she wrote short stories, poems, and screenplays. Always an avid reader, she stumbled across a book that ignited a deeper need for more and joined a fandom of like-minded individuals. Cecilia and her family relocated seven years ago to the great state of Texas, where she currently lives with her loving husband, wonderful son, and spoiled fur baby, Sadie. A lover of all things stories, especially those that are romantic, humorous and spicy, Cecilia Rene is always eager to pick up a book! For this reason, she will always give you a Happily Ever After.

Follow Cecilia Rene

☆Amazon US: https://amzn.to/3a5umLb
☆Website: https://bit.ly/3krehUG
☆Instagram:https://bit.ly/30DWh1S
☆Facebook: https://bit.ly/3ihR8lV
☆Twitter: https://bit.ly/30Dl71N
☆Goodreads: https://bit.ly/3hKEcIa
☆Newsletter: https://bit.ly/3ieZwCw
☆bookbub: https://bit.ly/3bERf8Y

Made in the USA
Monee, IL
14 January 2023